"Tanya."

"Yes." She hated the shyness that had come over her. Couldn't she wind back the hands of time and make things between them comfortable again? She'd have to go back to before she'd ever laid eyes on him in college, and she never wanted to have never known him. Even after everything she'd been through, meeting him was the best thing to happen to her.

"Sweetheart, look at me."

The butterflies in her stomach took flight, but she feigned interest in the occurrences of the busy city. She had no choice but to obey when he grasped her shoulders and turned her. Staring at his chest did nothing to ease her anxiety, so she took a leap and looked up into his eyes. Back to the brilliant hazel she'd always loved.

For every moment they stood gazing at each other she sank deeper. She could barely remember who she'd been when he hadn't been in her life for the past ten years. He was her world at that moment and nothing else mattered.

Her breaths came out in little pants as dread competed with

Dear Reader,

For some reason, the term "being on the down low" popped into my mind one day and refused to leave. That's the reason why Tanya Carrington ended up having an ex-husband who epitomized the phrase. It made for a fascinating and painful backstory for the heroine. The reintroduction of the man who rejected her years ago added to the drama that is her life.

I've been crushing on Miguel Astacio since I first introduced him in *A Perfect Caress* as the heroine's younger brother. Handsome, rich, fun, sexy, dimpled and always seeking the limelight, there's a lot more to Miguel than his partying ways. He's now put in the position to prove himself to his family, to the world and especially to the woman he gave up but now has a second chance to be with.

I hope you enjoy the story.

Nana

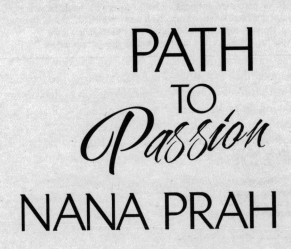

PATH
TO
Passion

NANA PRAH

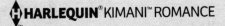

H HARLEQUIN® KIMANI™ ROMANCE

Recycling programs
for this product may
not exist in your area.

ISBN-13: 978-1-335-21680-9

Path to Passion

Printed in U.S.A.

Nana Prah first discovered romance in a book from her eighth-grade summer reading list and has been obsessed with it ever since. Her fascination with love inspired her to write in her favorite genre where happily-ever-after is the rule.

She is a published author of contemporary multicultural romances. Her books are sweet with a touch of spice. When she's not writing she's overindulging in chocolate, enjoying life with friends and family, and tormenting nursing students into being the best nurses the world has ever seen.

Books by Nana Prah

Harlequin Kimani Romance

A Perfect Caress
Path to Passion

To Ortanyi Arrington. Something about being the "wind beneath my wings" and a super fantastic friend.

Acknowledgments

I'd like to thank all of the people who have encouraged me with my writing over the years— you know who you are.

To every person who has ever read one of my books— thanks for keeping me going.

A huge thanks to Keyla Hernandez, Glenda Howard, Melissa Senate and everyone at Harlequin Kimani for your expertise and guidance.

To Hamzeh for your discussions on clubs and disguises that made the story even better.

As always I thank God for…everything!

Chapter 1

Miguel Astacio slid on his tailored suit jacket for the third time in twenty minutes, found the material irritating and flung it onto his seat. He hadn't been this nervous since... Well, never.

He went into his office's private bathroom to splash cold water on his face. Maybe that would take away some of the heat making him so unbalanced. Was he coming down with something? Maybe a case of food poisoning from the lobster thermidor he'd had for lunch? It would be a more comforting explanation than being panicked about seeing his best friend's sister.

Josh had called him a couple of days ago asking for a favor. His friend from college never asked for anything. The request hadn't even been for him. His sister was on the cusp of losing her nightclub and Josh claimed she needed his help. Miguel had no idea what he could do, but he'd at least listen to her story.

Tanya Carrington was the one woman he'd fallen irrevocably in love with back in college. He'd refused to acknowledge his feelings and had denied them to anyone who'd attempted to guess how much she meant to him. He'd already lost a couple of good friends in the past because he'd stupidly decided to date and inevitably dump their sisters. Lesson learned. When he'd been attracted to Josh's older sister after they'd first met, he'd stayed the hell away from her, or had tried to. When she'd insisted on hanging out with her brother, Miguel had had no choice but to get to know her better. The more he learned, the more he'd wanted her.

She'd been unlike any other woman he'd dated. Unimpressed by his wealth and status as an Astacio, she'd treated him as she did everyone else. Her genuine personality had placed her in a category above all others. He'd loved her chubby cheeks and on the rare times they'd hugged, her full curves had felt perfect against his body. He'd appreciated everything about her. Big mistake, because whatever had zipped between them every time they were together had threatened his much-needed friendship with Josh.

He and his soul brother had met in their sophomore year. Josh hadn't initially known Miguel was one of three heirs to the Astacio empire, and when he'd found out, it hadn't made a difference. At first, Miguel had been wary because everyone wanted something from him; after all, he wasn't just an Astacio but a Gill on his mother's side, which meant double the prestige, money and power. His parents owned a conglomeration of companies all over the world and kept creating more just because they could.

He recalled Josh's words on the day he connected his last name to that of the famous Astacio family: "I don't understand why you'd want to hang out with a geek like me, but if you don't mind catching some of my uncoolness, I don't mind sharing. Just don't expect me to be a groupie. I don't have time for that." His words had cemented their friendship. Miguel could never give up having such a supportive and loyal person in his life. The man's innate integrity and comedic nature had made him indispensable.

The splash of cold water against his face didn't help settle his nerves. Miguel wiped away the liquid and frowned at his reflection. Where had those sweat rings under his arms come from? *Dammit.* He stripped out of the shirt and stormed to the closet where he kept extra clothes.

He had to calm down. This wasn't the suave man he'd branded himself into since stepping out in front of the cameras with enviable confidence at the age of twelve. This nervous, sweaty man had to go.

Ten years had passed since he'd last seen Tanya. He'd been with more women than he could count during that time. Why the hell was he jittery about seeing her again? Sure, she'd been on his mind over the years and he couldn't help comparing every woman he'd been with to her, but he'd gotten over his best friend's sister. Right?

Momentarily distracted from his plight, Miguel smiled as he glanced at his watch and thought about how he'd used his marketing savvy to put the newly launched Astacio watch line in competition with established timepiece designers such as Movado and Breguet. Now people of prestige were wearing their Asombra watches.

Only ten minutes before her arrival. Pulling out a lavender shirt with a matching tie, he ignored the fact that it used to be Tanya's favorite color. What did he expect from her? To be the same sweet, intelligent, loyal-as-her-brother woman he'd spent all night talking to back in school? He scoffed as he slid the gold-and-onyx cuff links into the sleeves. She owned a nightclub. How sweet could she possibly be anymore?

The thought calmed his agitation. He'd changed over the years so it stood to reason she must've, too. Of course he'd become more handsome, confident, charming and responsible. If she'd headed in the same positive direction as him, then he had every right to fear this meeting, because other than being Josh's sister and two years his senior, she'd been damn near perfect.

Tanya Carrington had sat in her car for the past fifteen minutes willing herself to get out. Repeating phrases like "Turn off the engine. Unlock the door. Breathe, girl, breathe..." hadn't helped one bit. The heater keeping her warm in the harsh Cleveland weather could attest to that. Not only did she want to avoid the blistering wind, she'd become paralyzed at the thought of seeing Miguel Astacio live and in person again.

It was one thing to daydream about him after watching him give some speech or catching the entertainment news feature him with his latest girlfriend. He couldn't see how dejected she became every time his virtual presence crossed her world. She took a quick glance at the car's digital clock—in ten minutes she'd be walking into his office to ask for the biggest favor of her life.

Her heart thundered just as it had all those years ago when she'd first met him and every time after. Her brother's friends had never interested her. In college, her focus had been on her studies in order to keep the full scholarship that had allowed her to major in computer science at Ohio State University.

She'd been drawn to him the moment she'd walked into her brother's room and locked eyes with the new transfer. She could've sworn she'd seen an answering flash of interest in hazel eyes set in the most flawless light brown skin she'd ever seen. His long eyelashes had distracted her until he'd smiled and two dimples had appeared, making her knees so weak she'd sunk down into the first chair she could stumble to. She didn't know anything about him other than being the most handsome man she'd ever met in her life, but she'd known for sure that she'd wanted him.

While her nerdier-than-her brother had gone on and on about a sci-fi movie he'd just seen, she'd tried to pay attention, but Miguel kept stealing it. Not that he'd paid any mind to her after their initial introduction, where he'd tipped his chin up and said, "Sup," before ignoring her.

She'd spent more time in her brother's room those few weeks than she had in her own just so she could sneak glances at Miguel when he'd drop by. It took a while for him to warm up to her, but he had and they'd became friends.

Toward the end of their second semester, they'd

gotten really close, and she could've sworn he'd liked her way more than a friend. But every time she looked at him, she remembered the forty pounds she needed to lose before a guy like him would even consider dating her. How many times had she attempted to lose weight to be more attractive to him? Every time she'd started a diet, the pounds she'd lost would rebound when she fell into a state of temptation.

What she'd detested him for was the fact that he'd humiliated her when finally she'd summoned the courage to tell him she loved him just before she'd graduated.

Why hadn't she sought her best friend, Becca's, opinion on it before exposing herself? That's right, her stubborn self had already made up her mind and nothing would stop her. Becca may have told her to forgo the plan of revealing her true feelings for Miguel, which would've saved her from mind-numbing humiliation. Although the experience had left a lingering ache in her chest every time she thought about it, at least she never had to wonder how Miguel felt about her.

His rejection still rang in her ears. He'd never seen her as anything more than Josh's older sister and a friend as he dated every woman on campus. At least she'd had sense to tell him how she felt just before graduation. The timing saved her from ever having to see him again.

Tanya gripped the steering wheel and took deep, controlled breaths. No need to dredge up the past when there was nothing she could do about it. The focus should be on fixing her business so she wouldn't end up living in her car or, worse: moving in with her parents. In order to do that, she had to get out of the car, walk down the block to the fifteen-story Astacio building and ask advice from a man she'd once allowed to destroy her.

No big deal.

Chapter 2

The fact that her brother had suggested and arranged this meeting with the king of marketing had forced Tanya to drag herself out of the vehicle, smooth her knee-length down coat and speed walk to the Astacio building so she wouldn't be late. Just because Josh had had to convince her to attend didn't mean she was stupid enough to annoy the marketing director by being late. What had she been thinking sitting in the car for so long?

The trepidation and mortification she should've gotten over a long time ago had held her bound. She made it to the ninth floor of the building with one minute to spare. The space reminded her of what she'd learned about him over the years. The word *vivid* came to mind. Weren't offices supposed to be sedate and understated? No one must have given Miguel the message, because the reception area was the polar opposite of traditional.

Bright blues, yellows, greens and reds interspersed with white would've made teaching primary colors to a kindergartner fun and exciting. She blinked as she looked down at her conservative navy blue skirt suit with the maroon-colored silk blouse. She felt more than a little out of place.

She gasped as she turned to the right and saw what appeared to be a Jackson Pollock in matching colors to the office. Was it real? Just as she was about to step closer to the painting, the receptionist said, "Good afternoon. How may I help you?" His grin spoke of more than just politeness. He was amused by her reaction. His red suit and white dress shirt adorned with a canary-yellow pocket square fit right in with the trendy atmosphere.

"Hi. My name is Tanya Carrington and I have an appointment with Mr. Miguel Astacio."

"Please have a seat. I'll let him know you're here."

She nodded and sat, gripping her purse on her lap. For the hundredth time, she asked herself if she really needed Miguel's help. She'd been in worse situations than having her livelihood snatched away. When had she started lying to herself? She'd never been in such dire straits. Josh seemed to think Miguel could help, so she'd trusted him and consented to him calling his best friend. Besides, she'd transitioned into a confident woman who ran a restaurant and nightclub. Did it matter that it was failing miserably and she was spiraling into a near-debilitating debt?

"He'll see you now, Ms. Carrington," the stylish receptionist announced.

She swallowed hard with a longing look at the watercooler as she forced a smile to her face. "Thank you," she said while standing on shaky legs, making sure not to trip in her comfortable wedge heels. With the aim of going into the lion's den with a strictly professional mentality, she ran through a couple of her favorite affirmations. *I am worthy. I am great. I am successful.*

When she stepped into the large office to see the man who'd broken her heart with his callousness years ago, feelings of self-doubt rammed into her like a linebacker. One last thought rolled into her mind: *I am screwed.*

Miguel had lowered the heat, yet his fingers had difficulty grasping his pen due to the excessive sweat. He figured the busy look would be best when Tanya walked in. Unfortunately, a shaky pen due to his trembling hands was too telling, so he lay it down and waited for her to walk in while pretending to read a document.

The woman who entered could've been a swimsuit model with her full hips and breasts, emphasized by a slim waist. His gaze settled on her flawless medium-brown complexion and lingered. Her beauty stunned him. Large onyx eyes stared at him from beneath finely arched brows. Her light hand with the makeup emphasized her sculpted cheekbones and succulent lips. Who was this woman and where was Tanya? He watched the door she'd closed and waited for Josh's sister to follow behind.

"Good afternoon," the stranger greeted.

He started at the sound of the familiar voice, and

he snagged in a sharp breath. "Tanya?" he whispered. This gorgeous woman couldn't be her.

Her eyes turned cold although she smiled while extending her hand. "Good to see you again, Mr. Astacio."

The hard tone of her voice indicated otherwise. Pulling himself together, he ignored her hand the same way he did her lie. After how he'd treated her back in college, she'd probably never wanted to see him again, but at least he'd been honest. He extended his arms out to her, not missing the way she shrank away even though his smile was genuine. "There's no Mr. Astacio among us. Bring it in."

Instead of coming forward as expected, she stepped back, reached for his right hand and pumped it up and down.

Once again, the woman had shocked him. Everyone wanted a piece of him when he was willing to give it and yet she'd rejected his embrace. One thing hadn't changed between them, though. The zap of electricity that hit him had been present every time they'd accidentally touched.

Her eyes widened and her nostrils flared for a beat with her sharp inhale before she pulled her hand free. "It's been a long time."

Unable to get over how much she'd changed, he continued to stare, wondering why he'd never known such a transformation had occurred. What good would it have done to ask Josh about her when he'd made the ultimate choice to maintain their friendship instead of pursuing a relationship? They didn't run in the same circles so he never saw her. "You look amazing."

Shifting from one foot to the other revealed her nervousness. "Thank you."

"I'm being rude." He waved a hand toward one of the two maroon leather chairs in front of his dark oak wood desk. "Please have a seat."

She nodded, perched on the edge of the chair and crossed her legs at the ankles. Her long skirt suit exposed no skin. Most women who came to see him for a favor wore midthigh dresses and didn't sit as demurely. He wondered if he should be pleased or disappointed by her conservative demeanor. It would've been nice to see more of her legs. They'd always been beautiful.

His breath got stuck in his throat as their gazes locked. "You look amazing." Hadn't he said that already? Perhaps he was dehydrated from the excessive sweating he'd done before her arrival. "Can I get you some water? A drink?"

She opened her mouth to speak, but then shut it and shook her head. "No, thank you."

What had she been about to say? The woman he'd known in college had always spoken her mind, yet another trait he'd appreciated. And then he remembered that she'd come to see him because her nightclub was in deep financial trouble.

He strode to the refrigerator hidden within a dark varnished cabinet that matched the rest of the furniture, pulled out a bottle of water and downed half of it before returning to his side of the desk. How should he play it with her? Keep it strictly professional or treat her like a friend? Asking her on a long-awaited date was out of the question. Nothing had changed and he refused to ruin the incredible friendship with Josh.

Tanya was still off-limits. No matter how exceptional she looked or made his heart race.

She opened her bag and took out a notebook and pen. "Thank you very much for seeing me. I'll get right to the point so as not to waste your time."

Had her voice always been so husky? He'd remembered a lot about her, but not that. He nodded in response.

"It's no secret you're the marketing expert of your family's successful conglomeration. You can take any product, rebrand it and make it fly off the shelves." Her throat bobbed with her swallow, and he wondered if she was rethinking declining the offer of a drink. "You've done it with food products such as your chocolate puff cereal and malt drink, your children's multivitamins and quite recently, you've catapulted your newly launched watch line into the must-have category for the rich and famous. *Time* magazine said you had the 'Midas-branding touch.'"

Should he be impressed she'd done her homework? Once again, he had to stop comparing her to most women. She'd always shone above the rest.

For the first time since walking into his office, her smile seemed sincere. "You had the gift even back in college. Thanks to you, the football, baseball and women's volleyball teams got a whole new look from the money you helped them raise through getting students involved in fund-raisers. And when their looks changed, the next year so did their performance. It was nothing short of brilliant."

He hadn't realized she'd been aware of what he'd done.

Tanya continued her speech. "Toshia Covington

bragged about your role in reviving her party-planning business. She said if it hadn't been for you, none of her husband's money would've done her any good in providing CPR for her business. She said she would've pumped it in only for it to flow back out."

The clenching of his stomach didn't bode well. How did she know his sister's best friend? And even more disconcerting was how she knew he was the one who'd helped her. "Are you friends with Toshia?"

The hard shake of her head sent her thick wavy hair flying over her shoulders. "I've never met her. She gave an interview in *Black Women Entrepreneur* magazine and sang your praises." She crinkled her brow. "I'm surprised you didn't have people knocking down your door to tap into your branding acumen."

He chuckled as his body relaxed. The fear of stalkers was a real thing in his life, and he never took it for granted when someone had more information on him than they should. "I did. I had to take a trip to Argentina and then Jamaica to get away from the stress. Poor Franklin."

"Franklin?"

"My assistant. He absorbed the brunt of it." At her slight frown of disappointment, he rushed on to explain, "I rewarded him with a fully paid vacation to a place of his choosing once everything died down. And besides, I was scheduled to take those trips a couple of weeks later for business—I just happened to push up the dates." Why was he defending himself? She was supposed to be impressing him, not the other way around. After clearing his throat, he asked, "What can I help you with?"

She gained an inch when she straightened her back.

"Since you're an expert when it comes to reviving products which are sorely in need of rebranding, I was wondering..." Her eyes flicked to the left toward the view of the downtown Cleveland skyline and then roamed over the room until it reached him again with her mouth open.

He hid his amused smile behind his hand. Had she only just noticed this office? Would she comment or continue with her paused presentation? Most people noted the stark difference between his conservative decor and that of the reception area as they stepped into his office. She'd lost a point for not observing it right away. But then again, would he have noticed if he'd been in her position?

Seeming to recover, she continued her spiel. "Would you kindly give me some tips on how I can revamp my nightclub back into one of the happening spots in Cleveland? If it could become a hot spot in Ohio, that would be great. And if we could have people from all over the Great Lakes region coming to party there, that would be fantastic." She clasped her hands over the notepad and watched him.

He couldn't help laughing. She may have matured into an alluring woman, but her honesty and forthrightness of speech hadn't changed. He appreciated it more than she'd ever know. "Before I agree to anything, I have some questions for you."

How her whole body proceeded to stiffen even more was a mystery. Maybe she needed some time to get accustomed to him. He picked up his water and took a sip before resting his elbows against his desk in as relaxed a manner as he could convey. "How does a computer-science major who barely socialized in college because she was studying so much come to own a nightclub?"

At her loud gulp and widened eyes, he swore she'd jump up and sprint out the room. Her eyes then turned sad enough to clench his heart, and he knew that the next words out of her mouth would shake up his world.

Chapter 3

Even if Tanya had analyzed every picture she could've found of Miguel on the internet, she still wouldn't have been ready to meet him again live and in person. His persona claimed the space, swallowing her into his charm. She felt overwhelmed and drawn in at the same time. Only it wasn't where she wanted to be.

When she'd been sitting comfortably behind her desk at her nine-to-five computer-programming job, she'd found absolutely no joy in her work, but at least it had paid her on a weekly basis. She'd never appreciated money coming in at a steady rate as she did when it was no longer happening. When had things gone so horribly wrong in her life?

The moment Miguel had rejected her during her senior year of college. That's when she could pinpoint it to. The irony of coming full circle wasn't lost on her. Once again, he could turn her away, only this time she'd go without breaking apart.

Since he wanted an explanation before providing his much-needed assistance, she'd give him the truth. After living with the illusion of having a perfect marriage with her ex-husband, she was done with hiding. Besides, she doubted such a busy man would make the time to help her when he had a whole marketing department to run. How was he even able to party as much as the media claimed?

Her heart thumped hard as she assessed him. Miguel hadn't changed and yet he had. She thought he'd been hot in college. She'd been wrong. His body had filled out and his face had matured to the point of being devastating. The full head of curly hair she'd rubbed her hands through once, eliciting a moan of satisfaction from him, still beckoned her. Why had she listened to her brother? It had been a ridiculous idea to meet with him.

She picked up the notebook and jammed it into her bag, unable to be in the same room anymore without the memories flooding back and once again trampling her heart. To stop thinking about him, she took in the space of his office again. A dark expensive-looking desk, classic leather chairs and couches, all set off with a light peach–colored wall. The area was the total opposite of the waiting area and she wondered at the difference. Which one represented him?

Did it matter? She squirmed in her seat as unease refused to release its hold. She'd made a mistake coming to him and now she had to go. She'd exonerate her debt to the bank by selling her four-bedroom Victorian house that she'd paid off before the divorce.

Making it on her own sounded better than being slapped with the past every time she looked at him. Miguel should've been the man she'd ended up with; instead, she'd fallen into the arms of Broderick. Her ex-husband had set up the perfect marriage by making her lack for nothing. Not support, pampering, nor what she'd thought had been love. It had hurt to realize he'd used her. Her heart throbbed at what her life could've been if Miguel had claimed her in college.

Standing, she clutched her bag to her chest, hoping to suffocate the pain. "I'm sorry I've wasted your time, but thank you for agreeing to meet with me." She pivoted and walked toward the door. Before she could reach it, Miguel had sprinted across the room to block her path.

"What's wrong?" A shiver rolled down her spine. His voice had always been able to dig deep into her, eliciting a reaction.

She stared at his chest so he wouldn't be able to decipher her lie. "Nothing. I just figured out a way to get the club back into the black."

He hooked one of his elegant fingers under her chin and lifted her head until she looked into his eyes. His touch held her spellbound as her heart pounded with longing. Remembering who she was dealing with, she stepped out of his grasp and held on to the back of the chair she'd vacated so her weak knees wouldn't buckle and land her in a heap at his feet.

"Have a seat," he ordered.

She bristled. Who did he think he was? "No. I'm leaving."

"I don't think so." Miguel strode to his desk and made the leather chair squeak under his weight. "Are you aware of how much Josh told me about your situation?"

Her legs decided they didn't want to support her anymore, so she rounded the chair and collapsed. Her brother wouldn't have divulged *everything*.

The neatly trimmed goatee made a bristling sound as he rubbed it. "Josh mentioned you were at risk of losing the club you and Broderick had purchased together." His eyes narrowed the slightest bit. "You helped him and his partner, Jordan, to purchase the club by allowing him to use your house as collateral."

Was he judging her for wholeheartedly supporting her ex-husband's dream?

His light gaze held hers. "Under Broderick's management, The Palace thrived. I even went there a couple of times."

Her jaw dropped open.

"Why are you so surprised? We were on the same football team in college."

Her ex had kept a lot of things from her, but what did it matter if Miguel had come to the club? Maybe Broderick had remembered how she'd cried on his shoulder after Miguel had blatantly rejected her and didn't want to dredge up the horrific memories. It wouldn't have mattered because the memory was always a heartbeat away, tormenting her, even after all this time. She couldn't figure out why she'd never been able to get Miguel out of her mind and had stopped fighting it. Ten years was too damn long to hold on to someone.

Miguel opened a folder to reveal a graph with

colorful squiggly lines. He pointed to a low dip and tapped on it. "He'd kept the club in the black within four months of opening it and then six months ago things went south. What happened?"

Her gaze flittered to the hidden refrigerator as her mouth dried. Why hadn't she said yes to the water he'd offered earlier instead of letting her pride direct her answer? She didn't want anything from him, so if she could deny whatever he offered, other than his help to get her out of this muddle, then she'd decline.

May as well come clean about her shoddy ownership skills. Air filled her lungs with her deep inhale before she released it. "We got divorced and the club and house went to me."

His brows crinkled together and his voice lost a bit of its bass when he asked, "Why?"

Was the question regarding the divorce or the settlement? Did she need this embarrassment? Walking out would be easier. If she ran fast enough, he wouldn't be able to catch her, but she liked her home and wanted to continue living in it for the foreseeable future. "Because the house belonged to me. I had purchased it in my name long before we got married three years ago. When he wanted to start up the club, I believed in him and used the house as collateral."

He flipped his large hands over. She remembered the heat they'd elicited in her as he'd caressed her skin that night back in college. She shoved the thought away. "I don't understand. Couldn't he have paid you off? Or at the very least, you could've sold the club and split the profits."

Clasping her hands together until a knuckle cracked did nothing to remove the nervous flutter from her belly. What would he think of her? That she was a loser. A little white lie wouldn't hurt. "He insisted I keep it." Of course he'd said it in a sarcastic, challenging tone, but her prideful self had taken him up on it. It hadn't helped that she'd wanted him to suffer for ruining her life the way he had. How hard could it be to run a business? Not difficult with a background in finance and marketing, and six years working as the manager of a thriving club in Boston. Broderick had that experience; unfortunately, she didn't. Where he'd made their place fly, it was flopping under her incompetent control.

Miguel shook his head and narrowed his hazel eyes. "So you're saying that even though he'd poured his heart and soul into the club, he was willing to give it to you straight out?"

She twirled the strap of her bag as she struggled to maintain eye contact. His steady gaze had been her undoing every time she'd tried to lie to him. It turned out his eyes still had the same power of drawing out the truth when it came to her, but if she could hold on for a few more seconds, then maybe he'd be willing to let it all go. Seconds passed before the words spewed out. "I fought him for the club. With the help of my parents and my brother, I paid off his business partner so I could own it outright when the judge awarded me with it."

Before he could ask any more questions, she held up a hand. "It turns out that a woman can get almost anything she wants when her husband is unfaithful—" she paused for the dramatic effect the moment deserved "—with the man he divorces her for once he's able to marry him."

Her admission seemed to have knocked Miguel for a loop as he slammed his back into the seat and stared at her. Speechless.

At least she hadn't been the only one fooled by her ex. He'd been a master at hiding his homosexuality. "Now he's out of the closet and ecstatic. By the way, his business partner, now husband, is who I had to buy out and when I slid the check over to them, Broderick wished me the best of luck with a condescending 'You're going to fail big-time' snarl. He didn't think I could run the place. He'd told me so on numerous occasions throughout the divorce proceedings." She crossed her arms over her chest. His attitude had irked her to the point of spite. Just because she hadn't been able to keep him satisfied as a wife didn't mean she'd fail at the venture, even though her heart wasn't really in it. Pride was named one of the deadly sins for a reason. "I couldn't have him take away my chance at a family along with bursting my ego, so I decided to prove him wrong."

The room pulsed with the unstated words of her failure. To her revulsion, tears stung the backs of her eyes, and she tried to swallow the lump of disappointment, which had come from nowhere and refused to leave. She had to get out of there before she embarrassed herself even further. This time she didn't speak as she jumped out the chair and ran toward the door. She knew for certain now that coming to the man who'd driven her into Broderick's arms in the first place had been a colossal mistake.

Firm hands held her by the shoulders and turned her around before she could grip the handle of the door. When he pulled her in close, she pressed her hands against his chest and tried to push away. She really did, but ended up gripping the lapels of his suit jacket so she could rest her head against his broad chest.

For the first time since the night he'd destroyed her, she released the pain she'd been holding in. The sobs shook her body as he rubbed her back. She cried so hard that his words were lost on her, but the calming vibrations passing into her chest soothed. When the dam finally closed, she sniffled as the hiccups made their unfortunate appearance.

He released her and looked down into what must look like a monstrous mess of a face. Wiping the tears from her cheeks with the pads of his thumbs, her heart stilled when for the briefest of moments, he angled his head as if he was coming in for a kiss. Her captured breath burned within her lungs in anticipation, ready to relive his soft lips pressed to hers. Her nipples tightened at the prospect. Without warning, he stepped away.

Leading her to the couch, he sat her down and handed her a box of tissues. The unladylike sound that came when she blew her nose didn't make her feel any more comfortable. He went to the refrigerator, took out a bottle of water and twisted off the cap before handing it to her.

Tanya gulped the liquid to reduce the flame of mortification heating her head while she avoided his gaze. Had she actually thought he'd kiss her? She may have lost weight and looked okay, but he could have any woman in the world. Why would he want her? She'd never forget how he'd treated her.

"You must have really loved him," he said.

The water she'd just sipped slid down the wrong way, eliciting a sporadic cough. He actually thought the tears were for Broderick and the end of their marriage. If she wasn't fighting for her life, she'd have laughed. She'd thought she'd loved him and that their marriage had been good. No television show could've presented a more perfect one. Over time, she'd realized her love had merely been on a friendship level. Their marriage had been doomed from the start. Only he'd known the reason, though. Yet she'd also been at fault. Why had she ever attempted to give her heart to one man when it belonged to another?

His heavy hand banged on her back. "Are you all right?"

She nodded while pushing his arm away. "Yes," she croaked out, and held up a finger so he wouldn't call 911. "Just…need a minute."

The concerned man holding out his arms as if ready to catch her if she should faint was not what she'd expected after following the lifestyle he'd lived over the years. He'd recently calmed his partying, being seen on the celebrity circuit less frequently and dating women for longer than a week at a time, but even those few monthlong relationships never lasted and she wondered why.

The only thing the women he dated had in common was that they were gorgeous and all seemed to possess the same social rank. If the media were correct, he didn't look at race, culture or size when choosing his females. He'd dated Amelia Wilson and Sara Bloom, both of whom weren't just overweight, but obese. Her heart broke with each woman he'd been photographed with. Why couldn't he have fallen for her?

Not paying attention to his romances would've led to a happier life, but she couldn't fully release him from her world. And now here they were. Together.

She noticed the wet area on the lapel of his jacket and gasped. "Oh, my goodness. I've ruined your suit." She pulled out a wad of tissues from the box he'd given her and attempted to dab the area. As if that would help her save a garment that could probably pay off a month's rent on the club. It didn't ease her guilt to see that she'd gotten lipstick on the tie. She'd heard he favored Hermès.

"Don't worry about it," he said, gripping her wrist. "Besides, it's nothing my dry cleaner can't get out."

Every pulse point in her body bounded at his touch. With reluctance, she slipped out of his grasp. "Okay. I'll pay for the dry cleaning."

"That won't be necessary."

She waved her hands at his chest, remembering how solid and supportive he'd felt holding her. "But it's my fault."

Shaking his head, he grabbed her floundering hands and held them between his. "Really, Tanya. It's no big deal."

Ignoring the heat thrumming into her from his touch would require too much effort from her drained body, so she pulled her hands away and picked up the bottle of water from the table.

Once again, a softness returned to his eyes. What was he thinking?

"I'll help you get the club up and running."

Had she heard correctly? "I… I only wanted your advice. You don't have to help me any more than that."

"You know Josh even better than I do. The only

time he asks for help is when the situation is desperate. I can't let him down."

He and Josh had been close since the moment they'd met. It had taken effort to tamp down the jealousy she'd had of sharing her sibling with Miguel. "Thank you. But I'll pay you for your consultation."

He cocked both his head and brow.

"I don't have the money now, but with your Midas-branding touch, I'll be rolling in dough soon enough."

She had missed his contagious laughter over the years. "I still won't take your money. This is a favor to a friend. And his sister."

Tanya bowed her head to hide the sting. So they weren't even friends. Sure they'd spent ten years not speaking, but it sounded harsh for him not to acknowledge what they'd once been. She'd always wanted more from him, but hadn't been able to get it, so she'd ended up with nothing. Now they'd be working together. Would she be able to keep her heart locked up and safe? Did she have a choice? She looked up to have his glorious eyes fill her vision, and for a moment, her hands itched to hold his face still so she could feel his luscious lips against hers just one more time. Maybe the need for his touch would go away if she indulged her whim.

He nodded. "No argument for once? Good."

"I *will* pay you back," she vowed.

His grin brought out those delectable dimples. "Obstinate as always, I see."

Out of all the things that had changed, her stubbornness had probably gotten worse. "You don't know the half of it."

Chapter 4

Miguel got out of the most unobtrusive car he owned, a black Mercedes sedan, after parking half a block away from Tanya's nightclub. Her tears had shattered his heart yesterday. Making things better for her had been his only goal. If he could make her club a success, then he'd do it. No matter what.

Not only had she turned out to be even more beautiful than she'd been in college, she also had the inner strength to do anything she put her mind to. Something they had in common.

Holding her had felt right. Sure, she'd been bawling, but having her body melt against his brought back the memory of the incredible kiss they'd shared in college. The one kiss he'd compared all first kisses to. They'd all fallen short. Referring her to one of his outstanding marketing officers would've been the most logical action to take to rebrand The Palace, with the added benefit of keeping him away from her. Away from being enticed by her beauty and the temptation of leaning in to smell her light honeysuckle perfume every chance he could get.

While they'd been in his office, he'd fought his attraction to her and won. Who was he kidding? If it wasn't for the fact that she was related to Josh, he would've had her in his bed last night. Or at least tried to get her there. Normally running on instinct, he'd had difficulty reading her. One minute, she'd stared at him with the same desire in her gaze he remembered and his stomach would flip. The next moment, she'd seem to remember how much he'd disappointed her by choosing her brother's friendship over her professed love, and she'd become cold.

Both aspects of her intrigued him. That's why he should turn away from the cool metal door handle beneath his palm, hustle to the car and leave skid marks on the road as he raced away. A good sense of self-preservation would've had him doing just that. He opened the door.

The full house of patrons enjoying a meal in the downstairs restaurant piqued his interest. The club might be doing abysmally, but the restaurant conducted a brisk business. The tables were filled with people who may have felt too old to party the night away but who still wanted to have a good time in a trendy atmosphere.

The hostess didn't recognize Miguel in his disguise of a hat, full beard and stooped stature. He'd learned to be a chameleon over the past few months in order to be incognito in his personal life. His father's ultimatum still didn't sit right with him, but if he wanted the job of Executive Public Relations Officer, he had to stay out of the media as the poster boy of partying for at least another month and a half. His parents wanted to see that he could represent the Astacio companies in a responsible manner, so that's what he'd give them.

Did he need the position? With the trust fund being handed over to him when he hit thirty within the next six weeks, he'd never have to work again. Yet he couldn't imagine not working for a living. His parents had set an example and he meant to follow it. He didn't appreciate having to give up his partying lifestyle, or at least partying as Miguel Astacio. He'd developed aliases to keep the groove going without the media getting a whiff of him. He kept their interest by showing up at red-carpet and charity events because it wouldn't do to lose them from his tail.

He sat at a table, switched on his tablet and scribbled his observations. The restaurant might improve its patronage by serving microbrew. The waitress fairly skipped over to him. Someone loved her job. "Welcome to The Palace Restaurant. Can I get you a drink while you decide on your order?"

He smiled at the chipper young woman, enjoying the cool loft-like ambiance of the space. "Nothing to drink, but I'll take the house special to go."

"We have grilled rib eye steak and blackened trout fillet. Both are served with a fresh salad, potatoes and vegetables."

"I'll take the trout fillet, please."

She gathered up his menu as she bobbed on her toes. How much was Tanya paying her to do this job? "Your food will be out soon."

"Thank you."

Not telling Tanya he'd be stopping by gave him freedom to assess the place without her unique ability to distract him. He stood and trooped up the stairs to the empty second-floor club, took in the open area with a bar along each wall and then went up to the top floor to snoop around. He smiled at the thought of transforming the space into an exclusive VIP seating area. It would be perfect, considering the people partying up there could see down to the main dance level and be seen if they stood or danced by the railing. Otherwise, they'd have their own private party where the others would want to be but couldn't access.

He jogged down the stairs more excited than when he'd stepped into the building and sat at his table. The place had potential. And as the ideas formulated, he realized just how much of a success he could make of it. Of course it would take a heavy investment, but he'd figure out a way around that. Excited, he pulled out his phone to dial the number Tanya had given him reluctantly before leaving his office yesterday. How many times had he stared at the digits on his phone, wanting to call just to hear her voice?

He slid his phone into his coat pocket. He needed a plan before speaking to her again. Revealing to her how he felt wouldn't be a good idea, considering how angry she still was at him. Had he ever stopped loving her?

No. His feelings for her hadn't been enough to destroy a friendship with her brother.

Maybe he could treat her as if she were nothing but a sister. That might work, especially if he found someone to get serious about before they met again. He scoffed at the idea. It had been months since he'd dated anyone seriously, and he'd even use the term loosely. *Had consistent sex with the same person* would be more accurate. If two people date for months and the feelings don't deepen, can it ever be considered serious? He'd tried on several occasions over the past few years to become emotionally vested, but something always seemed to be missing with the women he dated.

The waitress set his to-go bag in front of him and he handed her the cash for the food, including a large tip. He left the restaurant, stepping onto the cold Cleveland street. The lingering effect of being taken by surprise yesterday by Tanya wouldn't rule him the next time they met face-to-face. Neither would his attraction to her.

Tanya watched the security monitor from her office and could've sworn she didn't breathe until Miguel left the vicinity. She'd frozen when she'd turned to face the CCTV screen and seen his stooped frame with his face hidden behind a fake beard and a hat. He hadn't called to inform her of the visit. What had he been writing so enthusiastically?

He'd taken it upon himself to help her improve the club, and she'd watched him as if it were all some sort of television show. Why hadn't she gone to see him?

Fear alone could take the blame for her inaction.

She dialed her best friend. "Becca, I'm so screwed."

"What's wrong?"

She rubbed the heel of her palm against her forehead. "I'm an idiot."

Becca snorted. "Is this about Broderick? How

could you have known he was gay? I definitely didn't. He had us all fooled."

Tanya stood and paced the perimeter of the space her ex had set up as an office. From the lushness of the black-and-white leather furniture, she'd ventured to guess it had doubled as his illicit love den. "For once, it's not about him. I went to see Miguel Astacio yesterday."

She snatched the phone away from her ear at Becca's shriek. "No. You will not do this to me over the phone. Either you get over here or I come to the club, where I know you are. You spend too much time in that place. Considering how dead it's been there, we'll have privacy either way."

"Not funny." But absolutely correct. "Let me make sure things are set up and I'll stop by."

"Bring a bottle of white zinfandel with you. Wait, we're talking about Astacio—bring two."

Tanya got off the phone thinking Jack Daniel's would serve her better. She tracked down her club manager to check that everything was set for the night. Clint Davis had recently been promoted to manager from bartender under Broderick a few months before he'd asked for a divorce.

Out of all of the people Broderick had been close to, Clint had been her friend, too, and she trusted him. He'd been supportive by providing more than one listening ear during the most difficult times after her divorce. While she'd been struggling as the new owner of the club, he'd proved himself to be loyal by working just as hard as her to return it to its previous status. None of their promotions, advertising or specials had had lasting effects, leaving them to flounder.

She popped into his office. "Hey, Clint. I'm headed out. Anything you need me to do tomorrow?"

In some ways, it was as if she worked for him. She'd paid very little attention to Broderick's involvement in the club, so she knew less than nothing about running it and it showed in the downhill progression of patronage. Clubs were more volatile than restaurants, and once people discovered that Broderick no longer owned the place, their numbers had declined. She lacked the ability to schmooze anywhere near as well as her ex. She'd prefer to be in flannel pajamas on a Friday night rather than speaking to strangers and making sure they were having a good time.

Her head throbbed with the thought of losing everything and dealing with the failure, but now that Miguel was on her team, soon she'd be the one bragging while raking in the money.

She still hadn't forgiven Miguel, but she could enjoy a man's powerful presence and comforting touch without liking him, right?

Clint's handsome light brown face looked up at her and his white teeth gleamed when he smiled. "We're good to go. DJ Slide will be here in an hour to set it off."

Tanya held back a grimace. The DJ wasn't her favorite. Slide liked to play only techno music, which Tanya didn't appreciate because she found it hard to dance to. "Do you suppose we could get someone else?" At Clint's narrowed dark-eyed gaze, she backed up a step. He didn't care for her opinion of DJ Slide and would always defend her saying she'd been one of the main reasons they'd been so hot for so long. She recalled Broderick hiring other DJs, but she'd rather slit her throat than ask him. "Not for this weekend, but maybe she could change up the techno with some house, reggae and Top 40 hits. Or stop playing the same twenty songs over and over again." She mumbled the last. Cowering went against her nature, but she couldn't afford to annoy Clint when she needed him most. Where would she get a trusted club manager if he left her?

"Nothing for you to do tomorrow," he said in a haughtier voice than she appreciated. "You've been here every weekend since taking over. Not even Broderick was here that much."

She stiffened. Was he trying to remind her of where her ex-husband had spent his time when he'd said he'd been at the club? No matter—their relationship had been doomed from the moment she'd left Miguel's arms and cried on Broderick's shoulder back in college. He'd been so understanding and had a way of making her feel good about herself. They'd stayed friends over the years and when he'd returned to Cleveland after working in the Boston club scene, he'd looked her up and they'd started dating. Three months later, they were married.

Everyone had told her she'd moved into the relationship too fast, but it wasn't as if she'd had a plethora of choices. The handful of relationships she'd had over the past six years had all gone nowhere. Broderick had liked her even though she'd outweighed him by sixty pounds and she would wince whenever he pulled her onto his lap.

"I'll take time off when we start making money again," she responded.

What was the expression that passed over his face?

He'd looked almost pained before grinning. Lately, something had been off about Clint, but she couldn't put her finger on it, so she blamed it on her distrust of all men.

"We'll get there," he affirmed.

She didn't quite feel his conviction as she nodded and pumped her fist. "Yes, we will. Have a good night."

"You, too."

She ignored the temptation to grab a bottle of wine from the club's stock so she could head straight to Becca's place. A quick stop at the supermarket wouldn't kill her. A brownie pick-me-up would be nice, too. No. Absolutely no brownies. She'd done so well to keep the stress eating at bay. Dealing with Miguel would not make her gain weight again.

She refused to let him have any kind of effect on her. She'd merely been in shock after not having seen him for so long. More like overwhelmed. Now that she had control over her reactions, she'd be able to deal with him to make her business successful. No emotion.

Chapter 5

Twenty minutes later, Tanya lounged on her best friend's couch with the crumbs of a decadent chocolate-chip cheesecake waiting for her to make them disappear. "So that's what happened." Becca had remained silent, sipping wine, as she listened to Tanya's account of her encounter with Miguel.

Becca poured herself another glass and bit off a tiny piece of her carrot cake. "You just watched him roam through your club and didn't even think to talk to him?"

"He was in some sort of disguise." She crinkled her nose. "Which I could see right through, but no one else recognized him. I don't think he wanted to be seen. And as I mentioned before, I was beyond embarrassed about what happened yesterday. I got snot all over him."

"Which is romantic as hell because he let you. I wish you could remember what he'd said as you were entwined in his comforting embrace. Maybe something like, 'Baby, it's okay. I'll be here to take care of you. You don't need to do it alone anymore. I love you.'" Becca said the last in a dramatic breathy whisper.

Tanya broke out into a fit of laughter. "You're a nut. I do remember an 'It's okay' being repeated."

"Do you think he likes you?"

Her lip curled involuntarily. "It doesn't matter." She and Becca had met in junior high school and had maintained their closeness even when they'd gone to different universities. "Need I remind you that I confessed my love to him, and he laughed in my face telling me to call him when I lost forty pounds. Sixty for good measure because he didn't like his women fat."

Becca rolled her eyes. "He did *not* say that."

"I know that's what he meant when he said he didn't want to lose his friendship with Josh by going out with me. I was too big a girl for him."

"You've always been too hard on yourself about your weight." Becca pierced her with a stare. "You were active, which made a difference in your structure. Sure you look great now, but you looked good back then, too. I believe him." She waggled her head. "I don't understand why he couldn't have both you and Josh in his life, but at least he didn't betray his friend by sneaking around with you."

Nothing her friend could say would change her mind about why Miguel had rejected her. It didn't help that although Broderick had been a wonderful husband for a while, she could count on both hands and feet the number of times they'd made love. She'd blamed the problem on her weight then, too. That time she'd been wrong. Tanya eyed the carrot cake she'd bought for her friend. Seeing the direction of her gaze, Becca broke off a piece slathered with frosting and handed over the rest. "With the marathon you're training for, you'll burn these calories off in a hot minute."

Tanya didn't say no to the offer. Tired of having a passionless marriage and needing to feel healthier, she'd worked hard a couple years ago to lose over eighty pounds. The ordeal with Miguel had had her eating like a fiend and before she knew it, she'd ballooned to the point where she got out of breath when walking from her bed to the bathroom.

The weight loss hadn't made a difference to the frequency or quality of the lovemaking with Broderick, and things started going downhill in their relationship. When Broderick presented her with divorce papers, she'd finally understood why he'd never really wanted to touch her in more than friendly ways.

"What am I going to do?" Tanya whined after finishing off the treat.

"Obviously, you're going to let him help you, but keep your heart as far away from him as possible. You married a gay man because of Miguel."

"That's not the way it went down."

Becca pursed her lips. "Would you have bumped into Broderick while crying your eyes out if Miguel hadn't rejected you?" She didn't wait for an answer. "No. You would've been more than happy to ignore him as you did every man you came into contact with because you only had eyes for Astacio. You wouldn't be at risk of losing your house and livelihood. Plus, you might have had the chance to find a guy worthy of you if you hadn't been attached to Broderick."

Tanya loved her best friend. Becca always knew what to say. "I wonder what he scribbled so furiously on his tablet. Do you think he'll be able to save the place?"

Becca sipped her wine, pondering. "He's a marketing genius. Josh did well by setting up an appointment with him. The only thing I'm worried about is him charming you into bed."

Tanya gasped with a slap to her chest. "I wouldn't sleep with him."

"That's my concern." Becca couldn't hold a straight face and giggled. "Seriously. You need to have a good time, and he might be the one to give it to you. Just don't get all emotional."

She ran a hand through her hair, refusing to consider it. "Girl, stop being ridiculous." At that moment, her cell phone rang. Miguel's name flashed across the screen. *It's him*, she mouthed even though the phone still rang.

"Answer it. And for goodness' sake, put him on speakerphone," Becca said.

She ignored her friend and hit Talk. "Hello."

"Hi, Tanya. This is Miguel Astacio."

As if she had more than one Miguel in her life. His voice melted over her, richer than the cheesecake she'd just eaten. "Hi, Miguel. What's up?" Was that her sounding cool?

Speakerphone, Becca mouthed.

"I stopped by your club this evening."

She thumped a fist to her chest to stop her heart

from hammering out of it. "Really? Why didn't you call me?"

"I needed to do a personal assessment. I did a walk-through and took some notes. I'd like to see the club in full swing. When is it busiest?"

Never almost slipped off her tongue. "Saturdays."

"Great. I'm free then. Please let your bouncer know to let in an Isaac Graham. I'll be incognito."

Her mouth flapped open and closed. What kind of costume could he wear that would be able to hide his lusciousness from the world? "Isaac Graham. Got it. But why don't you come as yourself?"

A grin filtered into his voice and she longed to see it. "I tend to draw a crowd wherever I go, and I'd like to see how things are on a normal night."

"Oh. Yeah. Of course."

"How's midnight? Things should be heated up by then."

Or not. "Sounds good. See you on Saturday. And thanks, Miguel."

"I haven't done anything yet."

"You and I both know you'll transform The Palace into a hot club again, so stop being humble. It never did suit you."

His laughter settled as a warmth in her belly. "I'll try to keep it in mind. See you Saturday."

"Bye." She waited until the line went dead before putting down her phone.

"No, Tanya." Becca stood in front of her wagging a finger and shaking her head hard. "No. No. No. No. No."

She hopped onto her feet so she didn't feel so small. "What?"

"You're already back in like with him. It doesn't matter what he did to you—you still like him."

"Cut it out. No, I don't. He's helping me."

Becca anchored a hand on her hip. "You made him laugh. I could hear."

She stared at her friend, waiting for clarification on her observation. "So?"

"Paired with your goofy smile, it's a sure sign that you like him."

Snatching up the bottle of wine, Tanya corked it and stalked to the kitchen. "Two glasses seems to be more than enough for you."

Becca followed. "I'm not drunk and you know it. I want you to be careful. He's never dated anyone for more than six weeks, and that's only happened recently. His life has been a revolving door of women. No matter what the media says about him now, he's a bad boy. Rich as hell, but still treats women as if they're disposable." She patted Tanya's shoulder. "He's already hurt you once. I don't want it to happen again."

She had difficulty shaking off the truth in her friend's words. The pain he'd put her through hit her squarely in the gut. She'd never be able to forget his callousness. He cared for no one but himself, and she'd just have to remember it as they worked together. "I'm a grown woman, Becca. I can take care of myself. Miguel is going to help me rebrand the club, and then he'll return to just being Josh's best friend who I never see."

Becca twisted her lips to the side and hummed. "Just be careful, okay."

"Always." Older, wiser and jaded, she'd be a fool to fall for Miguel again. He'd made her feel like an idiot once, and Broderick had done a better job of it than Miguel. The third time she'd be the one to end up on top.

Chapter 6

The thumping of techno blaring through the speakers set Miguel's jaw muscle twitching. Having never enjoyed jumping up and down rather than getting into a smooth rhythm when dancing, he hated the music. Dressed to hide his true identity, he'd texted Tanya when he'd reached the door.

The paparazzi loved him. He was the least shy Astacio when it came to making sure they spotted him. He'd readily compare himself to a Kardashian, only he didn't do reality-TV shows and he'd never be caught on a sex tape. Not that some of the women he'd been with hadn't tried. His sexual life had remained personal, no matter how many partners he'd been involved with.

Tonight, he'd worn a fedora with a smooth brim and adorned with a broad velvet ribbon. The full mustache made him look older than his twenty-nine years, but the dark contact lenses hiding his hazel eyes tended to unnerve him when he looked in the mirror. He'd darkened his skin with a touch of makeup, and the cheap polyester floral button-down shirt and trousers hid his love for expensive clothes well enough that no one, other than his family, could recognize him.

Taking the stairs up to the second floor, he didn't have to fight to make his way through the clubbers. The place had some college students jumping as if they were popcorn. A few older guys dotted the room, so he didn't stand out as much as he'd initially thought he might. He bobbed his head in time to the music and made his way to the bar. Ordering a scotch on the rocks, he glanced over his shoulder, wondering how Tanya had made it through the past six months without the business collapsing. How much money had she sunk into it?

The bartender gave him the drink and Miguel slipped him the payment with a tip. He almost spit out the liquid when he took a sip. Watered-down scotch wasn't his drink of choice. He held up the glass. Was there any liquor at all in the glass? After placing it on the bar, his breath hitched and his heart went crazy as he spotted Tanya. Damn, she was gorgeous, if not a little severe in her outfit.

She'd tucked a dark blue silk top into a black business skirt. Had she always dressed so conservatively? He couldn't remember. He'd been so excited to hang out with her back then that he hadn't really noticed what she wore. He cursed himself every day for messing things up with her.

His princess stood in front of him once again and

his hands itched to grab and hold her so close she'd only be able to breathe in the air he released. To kiss her like he had that first time, lips blazing as they melded into each other, her tongue sliding tentatively against his until he took complete control, teaching her as he relished her scent. Her taste. Her body finally being in his arms.

When they'd separated to suck in air, she'd professed the sweetest words of love he'd ever heard in his life. For a moment, he'd basked in it, but then the reality of who he was and what he had to lose dawned on him. He'd just kissed his best friend's sister, something he'd vowed to never do again. Josh would've seen it as a betrayal he'd never be able to forgive. So he'd confessed that he'd chosen Josh over her.

Her wide eyes had conveyed the blow he'd delivered. His heart had begged him to recall the words and tell her how much he wanted her, needed her, but his mind stayed in complete control. He'd turned his back on her and pretended interest in a book on his desk, unable to endure the tears in her eyes.

He'd heard rather than seen her stumble out the room as his heart broke.

It had been the lowest moment of his life, and he'd never apologized for his choice. Or comforted her with the honesty of how he'd really felt about her. She'd been the most beautiful woman he'd ever laid eyes on. She still was. Probably always would be. But he couldn't have her.

She'd never hear his words of apology. Not only wouldn't she believe it after all this time, but he didn't need her softening toward him. Having her like him and making him fall for her again would be detrimental for them both. It had been tough getting over her, and he didn't need a repeat.

Other than maintaining his relationship with his best friend, he was keeping her out of harm's way. His life was all about being in the public eye. She wouldn't be able to handle the spiteful women calling her vicious names just because she walked at his side. The media could be cruel. Even to him. He'd developed a tough skin, but it would crush her.

He waited to see if she'd recognize him. His heart stuttered the moment cognizance hit her and she grinned. For the second time in his life, she'd seen right through to him.

Despite being dressed as if he'd shopped in a thrift store, with a fedora covering his curly locks and his eyes darker than she'd ever seen them, she'd found him. He'd even shaved off his goatee and slapped on a mustache for the occasion. No one had rushed to the famous Astacio to become one of his groupies, so he'd fooled everyone else.

She crossed the floor to his side and leaned into him to shout in his ear over the blaring music. "Hi."

His crooked grin as he looked down at her flipped her stomach. "Sweet meeting you here. How's tricks, foxy lady?"

She placed a hand over her mouth to stifle her laughter. "I wonder if anyone knows Billy Dee Williams is in the house. With that mustache and darker complexion, you look like a younger version of him." He knew how to play a role and how to emphasize his most attractive features. His full dusky-pink lips brought to mind memories of when they'd made hers bend to his will, and without warning, she felt a need to taste them again. She sobered quickly. They weren't here to have a good time. Getting her out of debt was the name of this game.

Grabbing his hand, she ignored his delicious tingly heat seeping into her and led him to the stairwell. When he pointed upstairs, she shook her head rather than get closer to him and inhale his citrus and sandalwood cologne. Had the intriguing scent left her nose since she'd tried to huff it in after her tears had abated on Wednesday?

They took the stairs down to the restaurant area, where she'd intended to talk with him in her office. The club manager intercepted them with raised questioning eyebrows that annoyed her. She was a grown woman holding a man's hand—what business was it of Clint's? Nonetheless, she tried to slip her hand out of Miguel's and was surprised when he tightened his grip. Rather than fight him, she tried to relax. Easier said than done when shocks kept ricocheting up her arm only to land as a warm pulse of desire in her lower belly.

She cleared her throat as the men glared at each other. She recognized an alpha power struggle when she saw one. Too bad for Clint, because he'd lose against Miguel, who owned his manliness outright, and everyone who came into contact with him fell into it. "Clint Davis is the club manager. Clint, meet Isaac Graham." She was proud of herself for not stumbling over the lie.

The men shook hands for a brief moment and the tension seemed to build. "Welcome to The Palace, Isaac." Being so close to Miguel, he must recognize him, but he gave no indication as he emitted animosity.

"It's emptied out a bit since I was here last year." Miguel had changed his accent to a Southern drawl, but it didn't make the comment any less condescending.

Clint seemed to pick up on the slight because he threw his shoulders back and held his head high. *As if he could reach Miguel's six foot two inches of pure, poorly dressed, muscular body.* The man barely topped her five feet nine by an inch.

"We're in a transitional period under new management," Clint said with a nasty curl to his upper lip. Why was he being so defensive? He always blew off the slump when they discussed it.

Miguel didn't back down. "Aren't you the same manager from under Broderick's regime?"

How did he know? She tried to keep her mouth closed—she really did—but failed. She recovered before Clint did and tugged on Miguel's hand to drag him forward. He allowed it by following her instead of standing his ground.

In her office, she wrenched her hand from his and whirled around to face him. "What the hell was that about?"

"Why did you keep the same manager?"

She placed her fists on her hips. "Oh, no, you don't. Tell me why you tried to intimidate Clint and then *maybe* I'll answer your question."

He shrugged his broad shoulders. "He needed to be taken down a peg. The man thinks he's the king of the castle, forgetting that the queen is still alive and kicking."

"So you had to be a jerk to him? You do know

you'll have to work with him to get this club up and running, don't you?"

"I most definitely will not. First of all, he's your ex-husband's manager. The same man you said didn't think you'd succeed in running the club." He pointed an open hand at the video screen. "And, look, you aren't. A club doesn't go from hot to not, especially if the same manager is running it—unless he's horrible at the job or sabotaging you."

She backed away from the accusation. "He wouldn't. We're friends." She knew Clint to be a trusted confidant. He'd listened to her and hung out with her when she'd lain in the pit of loneliness after the divorce. He'd been so good to her. Like a brother. She couldn't imagine him doing anything to hurt her.

"Huh."

"Why would he want The Palace to fail? He'd be out of a job."

Uninvited, Miguel sat in her chair. Of course he'd take the most powerful seat in the room. "Unless he already has a gig lined up. Do you know that Broderick is opening up a new place?"

She fell into the seat across from him as the air left her lungs and her knees gave out. She hadn't spoken to her ex in a while, not that Broderick didn't try. Without fail, he called her every week apologizing for how he'd used her. If she ever spoke to him again, she'd most likely forgive him. After all, he'd been an ideal attentive husband in every way but sexually. Now she knew it had all been out of guilt. "How do you know?"

He came around the desk and sat beside her. "I make it my business to learn everything concerning the product I'm working with. I can tell you how much the club made monthly since its opening." He shook his head. "I hate to tell you, love, but I think your manager is an idiot. Granted, you aren't doing well, but things aren't as bad as you think."

Had she heard correctly? "What? How did you get a hold of our financial records?"

Miguel ignored her question. "Did Clint hire his whole family? The bouncer and two of the bartenders look like they could be his brothers. Even the female DJ favors him."

Tanya slid her hand down her skirt to keep from looking up at him. "Broderick promoted him a few months before he divorced me, and in that time Clint has hired a few of his relatives. Broderick didn't seem to mind so why should I?"

He grunted. "Nepotism."

Her eyes sparked at him. Was the pot calling the kettle black? He had no right.

"Don't look at me like that. My siblings and I worked hard starting from the bottom just like my grandfather made his children do. If we weren't qualified, we wouldn't be where we are now. Dad wouldn't have even hired us into the company."

"Oh." Her shoulders relaxed with the new information.

"If the workers and your manager were good, I wouldn't complain, but the bartender made me a drink that was so watered-down I felt hydrated."

She shrugged off his complaint. "I've brought friends to the club and no one complained."

"Of course they'd give your people the good stuff. You're the owner. Remember, I'm incognito. Last night, I sent my assistant in to scope the place out from a younger person's perspective, and he said the same thing about the drinks. He even spoke to a couple of the people there in order to verify that it wasn't a fluke."

She couldn't argue with what he'd observed, but she wouldn't be firing Clint or anyone else over it. He probably wasn't aware. Clint understood how much the success of the club meant to her. Besides, he'd be out of a job if the business collapsed. She'd discuss it with him and have him talk to the bartenders. "I hear your complaint and I'll look into it," she said stiffly.

Miguel rubbed his bare chin, drawing her attention to his full lips. All she'd have to do was stand and lean in and she'd— She took in a breath and dragged her gaze to his eyes, finding safety in them despite their altered shade. "What baffles me is why the restaurant is doing so well, but the club is tanking enough to bring it all down."

"I manage the restaurant."

She smirked as his whole body jerked back, pleased he hadn't gotten into all of her business. "Your intelligence didn't give you that little bit of info?"

"No. How is a computer geek able to run a successful restaurant?"

She frowned. He must not have cared enough about how she was doing over the years to ask Josh about her. "Ten years have passed since we've spoken. Do you really think I stayed the same naive woman I was in college?"

He had the good grace to bow his head after the chastisement. "No, but it would've been nice." He looked at her. "I liked who you were back then."

Stupid? Trusting? An idiot for love? None of it

mattered now. She had too much to do in the present and accomplish in the near future to dwell on the past. "When I graduated from college, I couldn't find a job as a programmer to save my life, but I needed money, so I turned to restaurant work. As I browsed the want ads for computer jobs on a daily basis, I made my way through the ranks from hostess to waitress, and after a year, I became assistant manager." She smiled at how hard she'd worked at that job and how much she'd loved it. "When I finally got work as a computer programmer, I had difficulty giving up my role as assistant manager. They were happy for the help and I was even happier for the extra cash, so it was a win-win."

She wished he'd take out his dark contact lenses. His eyes had always been expressive.

"I even took some restaurant management courses over the years because the field appealed to me. When Broderick proposed we open a club, I suggested a restaurant attached." She frowned as she recalled the argument that had ensued. It had been the most passionate they'd been for their whole marriage; unfortunately, it hadn't been for each other. "He didn't care for the idea, but since it was my home helping to back the venture, I insisted."

"Babe, do you know how difficult it is to run a restaurant these days? They're collapsing before they open." Miguel's face seemed to glow with pride. "And yours has even increased in profits over the past six months."

Did he realize how much the endearment and kind words melted her insides? She felt feverish and tingly all over. Standing, she walked to her desk and took her rightful place. Barriers were good things when she was around Miguel. "I handled everything about the restaurant from its inception. Now that I own everything, I have a more hands-on role. I comanage the restaurant with the original manager, which gives her more time to spend with her family. I've mostly left the club to Clint."

"So Mr. Slick manages it by himself?"

She gave him a warning glare. "Don't you start. Clint's a good guy and an excellent manager. Things are just tough right now. I wouldn't be able to manage the club. It's a completely different beast from the restaurant."

"I disagree vehemently about his management capabilities. Why do you give him so much control?" he insisted. "He's running the place into the ground for you, and if you don't fire him and his brood, even with my help, you'll have nothing to save."

She sighed, unwilling to believe that every man in her life was out to get her. A change of topic was in order. "What do you think of the place?"

He slid back into his seat and crossed a leg over the opposite knee with a slow deliberateness that told her their discussion about Clint wasn't finished. "Your chef makes great food and the one waitress I met almost gave me a cavity with her enthusiasm. There's very little I'd change about the restaurant, but have you ever considered specializing the bar as a microbrewery? I'm just thinking about what can give your restaurant a bigger advantage than what you have now. Microbrewing is popular now and it would bring beer lovers to the restaurant and maybe propel them to the club."

Her interest piqued, she listened with rapt attention as he explained the concept. For the first time since sitting down with him, she smiled. "The king of marketing strikes again. I'll do some research, but the microbrewery concept sounds plausible. Perhaps after the club starts making money again."

His double dimples appeared with his grin, making her mouth dry. A sudden need to be closer to him welled up inside of her.

"I'm glad you like it. Now for the bad news," he said as he pulled out his phone.

She held on to the armrests for dear life, not knowing what she feared more—his effect on her body, or how much his changes would cost.

Chapter 7

Maybe he should've waited and presented the necessary club adjustments to Tanya in the light of day rather than overwhelm her with the data after advising her to fire the club manager. He'd been so pissed she wasn't even willing to think about it that he'd given her the details of the needed changes without softening the blow.

Why wouldn't she listen to him about the man? He hadn't liked the way Clint had looked at her, either. As if he were in line to be her next husband. Although Miguel couldn't have her, neither would her smarmy club manager. He'd have him out of the club the first chance he got. Her friendship with the manager seemed to overshadow everything else when it came to the club. Business shouldn't have gone so far south under the same management, but she refused to see it. Tanya needed irrefutable proof that Clint was the cause of the nightclub's downfall. He'd get it, but it hurt that she didn't trust him.

With their history, why should she? He barely trusted himself where she was concerned.

"So what do you think?" he asked.

He'd emailed her the notes so she could read through them. Now she looked up at him from her laptop with a glassy look in her eyes. "How…" She glanced back at the screen and then at him. "It's a pretty thorough plan. Installing tinted Plexiglas walls on the third floor to create a sense of voyeurism-type privacy is a great idea for the VIP area, along with new, cozier furniture. I'm totally on board with hiring other DJs who will play less techno and a greater variety of beats. Upping our advertising to include not just radio but television commercials will definitely drive the people in here once all of your brilliant changes have been implemented." Her chair squeaked when she leaned back. "I can even get behind the name change. I was never fond of 'The Palace' when Broderick came up with it, but he never listened to my opinion about the club."

His blood heated as she gave him a wavering smile. She was just too beautiful, with clear skin marked only by a dark mole at the corner of her nose, angled dark eyes and full lickable lips.

"I mean," she continued, "I won't even be able to recognize the place when it's completed. Everything sounds incredible, but I may have to draw the line at the cages for dancers."

He thought she might. "Trust me, if we charge people to dance in them, they will pay. The one rule is that they have to keep their clothes on."

"We'll see." She stared at the screen again with her eyes unblinking "Um…" She rubbed the back of her neck and a light sheen of sweat broke out on her forehead. "How much will this cost?"

Now for the heavy convincing. He got up and stood beside her to point at the CCTV screen showing the dance area, which had filled up a little more in the hour they'd been going over his ideas. "I can see this place packed, people waiting all the way up the street trying to get in. VIP area filled with actors, musicians and pro athletes flying in to experience it."

Unable to resist, he leaned close so they were almost cheek to cheek. Her heat and honeysuckle perfume floated into him, and he turned his head so his starving lips could caress her one more time. He kissed along her jaw until he met the sensitive area of her neck, where he teased her with gentle nips until she moaned. She sprang as far away from him as the room would allow.

What had he been thinking? Why did she affect him this way? She took away his willpower like no other woman had ever done. Thinking became almost impossible when she was around. The desire to smooth his hands over her incredibly silky soft skin drove him to get closer, but he stayed rooted to the spot, watching her rub the goose pimples from her arms.

"Answer the question, Miguel." He was pleased to hear her voice quiver. "How much will it cost?"

He'd rather discuss the turbulent heat swirling between them, but if she wanted to ignore it then he should, too. "You've heard the saying that you have to spend money to make money, right?"

Her slow nod brought her hair forward. He watched as she brushed back the strands he wanted to filter his fingers through, bringing her close so they could fall into the attraction drawing them together.

Clasping his hands, he brought himself back on track. "As I said, with my visionary changes, this club could be one of the best in Cleveland's history. You came to me because I get results. That's why I'd like to invest in it." He really should've found a better way to deliver the news, but being around her flustered him to embarrassing proportions.

Her hands moved in wild, jerky motions before calming. "What?" she screeched, then paced the area near the door. "I don't understand what's going on here." Untucking her top, she fanned herself with the hem. Not seeming to do the trick, she sank into a chair and held her head in her hands.

He noticed the fridge and hoped it contained a bottle of cold water; otherwise, he'd have to run to the bar, and he didn't want to leave her alone in this state. He found a bottle, pulled it out, opened it and handed it to her.

She drank it all down. Clarity returned to her eyes as she glared at him with pursed lips. "No."

Not surprised at her answer, he knelt in front of her and stated the obvious. "You haven't even thought about it."

"What's wrong with you, Astacio? You were just supposed to take a look at the place and consult. I don't need a partner, and I definitely don't want you involved in my business."

The fact that she was still sitting there with him instead of kicking him out gave him hope. "Just read over the proposal and think about it. I'd only pay for the renovations. I wouldn't even be a true partner, just an investor, an angel investor, so to say."

"With a say in how my business is run."

"Only where the club is concerned until it's up on its feet, turning a profit like your restaurant." He reached for her hands and knew he'd made a mistake when she snatched them away before he made contact, stood and pranced away. Why didn't she react to him like other women? If it were anyone else, they'd be celebrating the joint venture with a round of sex on her desk. Not his Tanya. She had to hate him because he'd chosen Josh's friendship over the potential of what they could've been.

"I'm sure you can't take me seriously with this mustache and hat on, so I'll leave and give you time to think about it."

Her narrowed eyes sent a chill down his spine. "I'd rather go groveling to Broderick asking him to be my partner than to have you invest in the club."

He held up his hands. "That's a bit extreme, isn't it?"

"Is it?"

He averted his gaze, intentionally losing the stare down when he noticed not only the anger of her scowl but the sadness in her eyes. He cursed his young self for having hurt her. Would it have been a horrible thing to have been honest with her at the time?

To tell her that Josh would've ended their friendship if he'd even contemplated trying to date her? It had all come up during a conversation about their siblings. Miguel had always been protective of his sister, Lanelle, even though she was older, so he could understand where Josh had been coming from when he'd made the threat. Additionally, Josh was one of the few people in his life who had never tried to use him for his fame or money, and he'd made the hardest decision of his life and chosen his friend over a potentially great—or disastrous—love affair with Tanya.

Did any of it matter anymore? He'd hurt her, and from that there was no turning back.

He opened the door, letting the annoying techno music into the room. "I'm sorry for how I treated you back in college. Things were crazy, and I was young and a mess." He pounded a fist on the door. "I should've handled it better."

She lowered her gaze, but not before he witnessed the glimmer in her eyes.

God, his heart ached. Even more than that night he'd turned her away. At least then he'd had the knowledge that she'd loved him to hang on to. Now she hated him and there was nothing he could do about it.

He stood his ground as his throat tightened. She didn't need his comfort, no matter how much he wanted to give it to her. She'd walked into his office seeking his expertise. She wanted to make her business thrive, so that's what he'd help her do. He owed it to her. If only she'd allow him to implement the plan. "Please consider the offer," he choked out before leaving and closing the door behind him.

Chapter 8

"Josh, I'm coming over." The futility of the words as Tanya spoke with her brother on Skype wasn't lost on her, but she needed his presence. A night of crying after Miguel's unexpected apology hadn't helped. Her head felt foggier than when he'd slammed all the changes he wanted to make to the club at her and then offered to invest.

Other than his advice, she wanted nothing from the man. Especially not his money or the tingles he'd elicited with his soft lips against her sensitive skin. Definitely not those.

Becca had been absolutely no help during their early-morning phone call. Her friend had told her to take the money as compensation for the psychological damage he'd caused back in college.

Josh shook his head. "You do realize I'm still in The Gambia, right?"

Her bridge-building engineer brother was never where she needed him to be. He was always roaming the world, and she missed him. Although he was younger by two years, she relied on his old-soul wisdom. No one knew her like him, not even Becca, even though Tanya didn't always tell him what was going on in her life. "When are you coming back?"

"I know that's not why you called in the middle of night. You hear that?" He craned his neck toward the darkened window. "Silence. Not even the damn roosters are awake yet. I'm four hours behind you. I wish you'd remember that when you call. What's up, Tee?"

She looked at her computer's clock. Not even eight, yet. Oops. "This is an emergency." She explained how much work the club needed, Miguel's opinion of Clint and how he wanted to make things better. She left out the part about how he'd made her want to melt into him and kiss every inch of him even though he'd destroyed her ten years ago. "What am I going to do?"

"First of all, don't let your stubbornness get in the way."

She stuck out her bottom lip. "I'm tenacious."

"Whatever. Put it to the side for once and look at the facts. Give it a shot. Miguel is the best at what he does. That's why I called him for you. You would've let your business sink to the point of no revival and I couldn't have you homeless. Or, worse, living with Mom and Dad." He chuckled. "Dad's anal retentive tendencies would drive you up a wall."

A smile crept onto her lips. She loved her parents,

but living with them again wouldn't be good for her mental health. "So you think I should let him invest?"

"Let's look at the facts. First of all, I think Miguel is right about Clint." He held up a hand to stop her argument. "I know you consider him to be a friend and he was there for you during the divorce, but it doesn't mean he's a good manager. How could your restaurant do well under yours and Eva's management, while the club is flailing under Clint's? Something's not right."

Her finger sprang into the air. "Speculation and proof are two different things." She refused to believe she'd been wrong about yet another man in her life. It was as if her instincts had fizzled out completely.

"Then get some. Go over the books. Clint's had free rein over the accounts since Broderick left. When was the last time you checked them?"

She crinkled her nose. She hated the financial aspect of running a business and only did it for the restaurant because she had to. Her ex had been a genius at it. "I'll have my accountant go over them."

"After discussing it with Miguel last night, we decided—"

"Hold up." She narrowed her gaze at her little brother. "You talked to him?"

He blinked as if he'd just realized what he'd said. "Don't take this the wrong way, but you aren't the most logical person when he's around."

Her head jerked back. "What do you mean by that?"

"Deny that you had a huge crush on him in college, and I'll call you a flat-out liar."

"What?"

"You heard me. Everyone who was in the same

room with you two knew. But I warned him to stay the hell away from you or face the consequences."

The tightness in her chest made it a struggle to drag air into her lungs. She rotated the chair in her home office away from the screen to give her a chance to gain some understanding. When she turned back around, her shock had morphed into anger. "So what if I liked him back then? He didn't return the feelings. I'm in full damn control when I'm around him and I don't appreciate you discussing me behind my back with him. He may be your best friend, but I'm—" she jammed a finger into the center of her chest "—your sister. You'd be better off remembering that."

He relaxed into his seat as if they were having a lovely conversation over tea. "Always so dramatic, aren't you? So much like Dad. No wonder Mom calls you his clone."

"Oh, shut up." She looked up at him through her lashes. "By the way, Miguel never liked me."

Josh snorted. "What planet were you living on? The boy adored you."

She didn't believe him. Her brows scrunched together. "Did you say you told him to stay away from me?"

"Damn straight. He wasn't ready to be with you. He would've crushed you."

He did it anyway.

"Do you remember the circumstances that made him transfer from Stanford University to Ohio State his sophomore year?"

Still too upset to speak, she nodded.

"I didn't find out until a month after we'd become friends, and even then it was from his perspective.

After some digging, I found out it was true." Josh told the story as if lost in the memory.

"During his freshman year at Stanford, he'd been wild. From what I hear, coed living after attending an all-male boarding school can be overwhelming. He had more women throwing themselves at him than he knew what to do with. During his second semester, he met up with one who wouldn't tolerate being part of a harem and told him to make her his only. When he refused, she claimed he'd raped her."

"It wasn't true."

"With his lifestyle back then, not everyone believed the same. A full-fledged investigation took place and the tabloids had a field day."

"I remember hearing about it months later. How come I wasn't in the loop earlier?"

"You never watched the news. If the topic wasn't about computers or school, you didn't pay attention. That's why I liked Miguel's influence on you. He helped make you a more aware, well-rounded person.

"In the end," Josh said, "it all came out that the woman was lying, but by that time, things had gotten bad for him. His father ordered him to transfer into his alma mater, to which he'd made huge donations over the years. When the students at Ohio State found out about what had happened, they initially shunned him."

"But you stood by his side."

"Of course. Once a friend—"

"Always a friend," she finished for him.

"Unless they muck things up."

She inhaled deeply before releasing the air. "Like hurting your one and only sister?"

"That's on top of the list."

She felt the same about him. They'd been close all their life and she couldn't see anything changing that. "Would it have been all that bad for us to get together?"

He angled his head, studying her. "At the time, yes. He wasn't in a good place. He'd been in a near miss that had almost destroyed his life, and he still needed to find himself. He wouldn't have been able to commit."

What about now? She wanted to ask, but what would be the point? The hurt still lingered and she doubted she'd ever be able to trust him again. "So you think I should take his offer?"

"Definitely. What do you have to lose? He told me he'd have his sister go over the books for you."

Her mouth gaped open. "She will not."

"That's what he said. Something about owing him for showing up at her fund-raisers."

Tanya had never met the woman, but Miguel had spoken about Lanelle often enough to show how much he respected and loved her. She hadn't heard anything about the reclusive heiress in the media over the years, but it had been announced last year that the Astacios' only daughter had given birth to a healthy baby girl. She could only imagine Miguel's joy at being an uncle.

"He could get anyone to check the club's finances. Why her?"

Josh shrugged. "He trusts her."

"Oh." She had a lot to think about. "I'll let you get some sleep." A loud crowing reached her side of the Atlantic.

"Too late for me. What are you going to do about

the offer? You're not a stupid woman, so I know you're going to take it."

"You'd better watch it, little brother. Don't think you can overstep your bounds just because you're a bigwig in the bridge-building world."

He chuckled.

"I'll think about it."

"Don't think too long. Your profits are dropping. Besides, the place needs to be ready for Miguel's thirtieth birthday bash in a month."

"What?"

His eyes went wide. "He didn't tell you?"

"No."

"You two really need to sit down and talk. Just remember to put your *tenacity* aside. I love you, sis. Be good."

"Love you, too. I'm always good."

He hung up laughing.

Too much had happened within the past week. Meeting up with Miguel had been the most overwhelming. She had to figure out what to do about him. If they ended up working together, she'd have to find a way to safeguard her heart from his charm. If she decided not to take his help, she'd need to dig up enough patience so she'd be able to live with her parents. Oh, the choices.

Chapter 9

After another night of the club being less than encouraging, Tanya had called Miguel on Sunday morning. Holding on to her pride shouldn't cause her to lose her livelihood. Right after uttering her greeting, she'd found herself invited to dinner so he could review the presentation because he said he'd botched it up the first time.

Before she knew what had happened during that short phone call, she'd been told he'd pick her up at five. Dizzy, she'd heard the click of the phone disengaging as she tried to figure out what he was up to.

She'd have to wait six hours to find out because he wouldn't tell her until he was ready. He'd always been like that. Just as determined as her if she remembered correctly. She'd argued more with him in those two semesters than she'd ever done in her life.

He'd later admitted that he enjoyed their lively discussions because he'd rarely met a woman who would disagree with him. Once the females found out he was an Astacio, they became all giggles. He said he'd liked that she gave her true opinion without caring how he reacted. They'd discussed everything. From poverty to racism, clothes and even sex, although she'd had little to contribute to the subject.

Not every conversation turned into a heated debate, but she didn't mind when they did because they always ended in a respectful agreement to disagree.

No one had ever been as engaging to converse with. She'd learned so much about other cultures from his travels all over the world with his parents. It had impressed her that he wasn't in the least bit spoiled although he had really expensive taste.

They'd been great friends before she ruined it by kissing him a few days before her graduation. The temptation had hounded her since they'd first met, but he always seemed to have a girlfriend, which had upset her more than she'd let on. Why couldn't she have been the one on his arm at the school's winter wonderland dance? Or sat next to him at the football awards dinner?

Having a business dinner with him would have to suffice because there could be nothing more between them. Sure, she'd lost lots of weight and looked all right, but she wasn't as beautiful or rich as the women he tended to date.

Their lives were worlds apart. He was dogged by the paparazzi and had to wear a costume so they wouldn't catch him. She enjoyed coming and going at her leisure without having to watch over her shoulder for who was snapping pictures of her wider-than-it-should-be behind.

With all of his money, she'd never fit into his luxurious world. Give her a Miller Lite with some chicken wings, blue cheese dressing and celery sticks, and she was a happy girl. She could only imagine the kinds of fancy dinners he had where she wouldn't be able to pronounce the names of the dishes.

Was she actually thinking about him as more than someone to help her get the business back on its feet? No. She'd been there once and never needed to venture into that terrain again. It didn't matter that their one and only kiss had set her world upside down and her body ablaze. That she could still feel the softness of his perfect lips as he'd sucked gently on her bottom lip, then his tongue sliding into her mouth and making her toes curl.

Picking up a magazine from the coffee table, she fanned herself. Nope. Never again.

Tanya held on to the driver's proffered hand as she got out of the Jaguar. The sleek, low-slung vehicle had purred on the way over, making her wonder if she needed to change the muffler in her Camry because her car definitely didn't sound like Miguel's. She'd been disappointed that he hadn't been in the vehicle when it had stopped at her front door and he'd called to tell her it had arrived.

The butter-soft seats had conformed to her body, and she'd never wanted to leave the elegant interior. The vehicle had transported her to Pepper Pike, a suburb of Cleveland where only the wealthy could afford to reside. She hadn't closed her mouth or eyes since entering the area. The homes closer to the road were beyond gorgeous. She loved her old Victorian, but no one would have to persuade her to live in one of these ostentatious buildings.

They'd turned off the main road, climbed up a winding hill and arrived at a closed gate. The driver had placed his hand over an electronic pad and the intricately designed black metal had opened for him to drive through. It took them a few more minutes of climbing to reach the driveway of a stunning house that snatched her breath away. A two-story wooden structure surrounded by forest. The place seemed to blend into its environment and stand out at the same time.

Miguel opened the door with a flourish, wearing navy blue trousers that no other man could make look as good along with a dark green-and-blue-striped button-down shirt. In her favorite black suit, she felt dowdy next to him. "Welcome to my home, Ms. Carrington."

Still not having recovered from the brilliance she'd witnessed on the way there, she quipped, "What, no maid?"

His chuckle sent a thrill through her and she shivered. "She's in the kitchen helping the cook to finish up. I wanted the food to be perfect for you. Come in and get warm."

Had he been that attuned to her that he'd noticed how she'd reacted to him? She stepped into the marble hallway and tried really hard not to be impressed with the chandelier, gigantic bouquets of fresh flowers on what appeared to be an antique table, gleaming wood banister leading to the second floor. Was that an original painting done by Bernard Vera, a local artist who'd recently become sought after? "You know I would've been happy with hot dogs and beans."

He proffered his bent arm to her. She hesitated for a moment before hooking her hand into the crook of his elbow. Her heart raced at the contact and she wasn't even touching his skin. The idea hit her to turn around, hijack his gorgeous car and never see him again. Not a realistic scenario. Besides she was enjoying getting back into the friendship they'd shared.

"I'm offering you a tour before you start begging and pleading for one."

He grunted when she poked him in the ribs with a finger from her free hand. "Not on your life. I would've just asked to use the restroom and accidentally found myself lost." Glancing around, she doubted she would've had to pretend. The place was enormous. The living room through the first door on the left was big enough to fit everyone in her large extended family without anyone annoying the other. The luxurious white-and-tan furniture wouldn't have survived her little cousins, though.

To the right, a few feet down the hallway, was another living room. This one seemed more lived in with its olive green, warm browns and friendly cream furniture. Books filled every inch of the shelves along one wall. She remembered how much he had enjoyed reading. While she'd been focused on her textbooks, he'd had a novel in his hand. Must've been nice to be so naturally intelligent that he didn't have to study all the time.

She'd learned to appreciate reading for pleasure once she'd gotten married and had given up her part-time job at the restaurant in order to spend time with her husband. Who knew books could be more of a companion than her spouse had eventually proved to be? She refused to let thoughts of his lying, cheating ways into her life for another moment.

A full dining room, four bedrooms—minus his, which she'd longed to see, but he'd skipped over with barely a mention—and a basement with a game-and-gym-combination room later, they stood at a nook in the kitchen with a table set for two. "Your house is beautiful. Not the bachelor condo you bragged about back in college."

The gentleman he'd always been pulled out her chair and she sat. "I have one of those, too. In the city."

"New York?"

He chuckled as he passed her a bowl filled with salad. "I meant Cleveland. Sometimes I'd prefer not to commute out here."

Scooping out the vegetables, she asked, "Why? I'd never leave the place."

She glanced up just in time to catch his expression. Was that longing on his face? She placed the bowl on the table and picked up a bottle of dressing. "Can I ask you something?"

"No, I don't have a girlfriend or concubines."

Her hand tipped the bottle too far over and she ended up with an overabundance of dressing in her bowl. Her shoulders relaxed at his laughter as he switched salads with her.

"That wasn't my question."

He started in on his salad after bowing his head for a silent prayer. The move touched her. Her parents had always taught her the importance of being grateful for the food she ate. She did the same, then ate a forkful of greens before asking, "Why is there such a stark difference between your office and the reception area?"

Once again, his laughter lifted her spirits. She could listen to it all day. Those dimples didn't help. She'd never gotten a chance to kiss them during their single foray into romance. Her face heated at the direction of her thoughts and she rushed out her explanation. "I mean, if I were to guess, from the style of your home, your office—which reminds me a lot of the picture I once mentioned I wanted my future office to look like back in college—is the style you prefer."

"If you recall, I ripped out the page from the magazine and told you I'd decorate my office that way before you had the chance because I liked it even more than you did."

She pursed her lips to keep from smiling. "I remember you being a copycat and liking all of my ideas."

He waved a fork in a negative gesture and smiled. "It's just that we had a lot in common."

Suddenly feeling playful, she asked, "How do you know I wasn't faking it?"

"Sweetheart…" His voice took on a husky timbre that sent her belly quivering. "I have a natural gift for knowing when a woman is faking." The tension hung in the air before he said, "Besides, I always let you give your opinion first."

She thought back on a few of their conversations.

"Stop thinking so hard," he teased. "I was slick about it. That was until I got to know you better. And then it became an equal party. Anyway, I once offered

my assistant anything he wanted for saving my hide
from my parents when I'd missed an important meeting after a night of indulging a few years ago. Franklin
can be ingeniously convincing when he chooses to be.
Lucky for me, because my dad would've kicked me
out of my position if he hadn't been. Franklin chose
to decorate what he considers his office."

She pushed her empty salad bowl to the side.
"When I first walked in, I thought it was you who'd
had it decorated. It seemed to suit you."

"Young me."

"What?"

He got up, went to the oven and pulled out two
dishes with the oven mitts he'd put on, making him
even sexier in a domestic way. After placing them on
the table, he flung the gloves back onto the counter.
"The younger version of myself would've done it if
my parents had thought of me having an office. Cu-
bicles with the other workers as I climbed my way up
the ladder of experience was more what they had in
mind. I've matured since then." He looked her in the
eyes. "I've grown."

Okay. No subliminal messages there. She glanced
down at the plate of roast beef, twice-baked potato
and grilled vegetables he'd set in front of her. "This
looks amazing." She took a bite of the tender meat
and had to hold back a groan of pleasure at the flavor. "Now give me the incredible presentation you
think will influence me enough to allow you to invest. Don't forget the part about your birthday party
being held at my club."

He set the forkful of food back on the plate before
it could reach his mouth. "You spoke to Josh."

"He *is* my favorite brother," she said, spearing a piece of cauliflower. "I asked his opinion."

He arched one of his amazing brows. "And...?"

She gave him her most mischievous grin. "Sell it, Astacio." She'd always enjoyed teasing him, and it seemed it was another thing that hadn't changed between them. Once they started working together on her club, she'd have to distance herself. If she got any closer to him, she'd end up falling in love again. Which mean she'd also end up hurt and alone.

Chapter 10

The words "Pay you back in full with interest" caught Miguel's complete attention as Tanya went through the rules of their new business arrangement. As they'd eaten dinner, she'd transitioned slowly from the cold, wary woman who'd met him in his office a few days ago to the bubbly, confident one she'd been back in college. He'd become enthralled with her. Lost in her eyes and he wanted her.

Josh and their friendship be damned. If once again put in the position to choose between the two Carringtons, he'd pick Tanya. He cherished his friendship with Josh, but he knew Tanya was his future. He wasn't the reckless, fun-seeking boy he'd been back then. As he'd told Tanya earlier, he'd matured, although it had taken years of getting into tons of trouble and embarrassing his family. Sometimes the media still painted him as the same type of player he'd been back in the day, but overall, he'd grown into someone worthy of her.

If only she'd get a case of amnesia about both that wretched evening and how much she'd loved Broderick. His hand fisted at her caring enough about her ex to bawl on his shoulder during a business meeting. He'd make her see that he'd never again do anything to intentionally hurt her.

"Back up a minute." He held up both his hands to stop her diatribe. "I won't take interest for this venture. I'm helping out a friend."

"And Josh appreciates it, but I can't take your money knowing you could be making more somewhere else."

So she no longer saw them as friends? He couldn't really blame her, but it didn't stop his stomach from twisting. "I was talking about you."

Her large eyes glanced down so he couldn't read them. "Oh."

Time to apologize again for ruining the best thing he'd ever had in his life. He shifted closer to her on the couch where they'd shared dessert. He lifted her chin with his finger so she wouldn't miss the sincerity in his eyes. Beyond anything, he needed her to believe him.

She'd once told him that his eyes were the most expressive part of him. "I still consider us friends, Tanya. I was young and stupid, and I hope you can forgive me for hurting you so grievously. I didn't mean to reject you by choosing Josh. I got scared for more reasons than I could ever say." He tapped his chest at the area over his heart. "You were and always will be spectacular to me. No one else has ever made me laugh to the point of tears, frustrated me to the precipice of confusion or allowed me to be my true self around them."

Unable to relinquish his finger from the electrifying softness of her skin, he rubbed his thumb over her chin. The sensuality of the moment churned between them and his body longed to shift closer. To caress her cheeks, draw her into his arms and press his lips against hers in a way that would leave no doubt in her mind about how much he respected and wanted her. Rather than ruin things between them before they could start, he released her, keeping his gaze glued to hers. "Will you forgive me so we can be the friends we once were? No. Even better friends, because we both have more to offer now than we ever did."

Her throat convulsed with her swallow as she stared at him; for once, her face remained neutral and he couldn't read her. Would she reject his long-overdue olive branch? It really didn't matter if she did. He had more apologies stacked and ready to offer. He wouldn't give up on her. Not again.

The old pain didn't roar to life as Tanya listened to the apology. Would it make her a sap to forgive him? The man she'd been in love with, had exposed her heart to, had stomped her down to the point where her strength and confidence had to be reconstructed from the ground up. It had been difficult, but she'd done it. Could she forgive that?

She'd missed his friendship over the years. More than once she'd wondered what he'd think of an issue and then mentally slap herself for the errant thought.

He'd had no right to anything in her life. Now he sat before her, offering yet another apology, this time with a proposal of friendship.

She'd loved him so hard back then. The first and last man she'd felt so deeply about. Not that she hadn't tried with Broderick, but circumstances had made it impossible. The other men she'd dated had been experimental at best. Her heart always returned to the one who'd shunned her, and for a time, she'd hated herself for it. But not anymore.

Rising as a new woman from the ashes she'd been, she saw the opportunity his friendship presented and she wouldn't turn it down. "I accept your apology."

His gorgeous light eyes blinked repeatedly. "But don't you want me to cut off all my hair first?"

She giggled as her fingers flexed to avoid running her fingers through his lustrous curls. "No."

"To streak through downtown Cleveland?"

The image of him running naked appealed to her, but she shook her head. "If memory serves me right, you did that in Cancun during spring break. The tabloids had a field day with it. Your behind was everywhere."

"Stupid dare I was too drunk to turn down. My father tore me a new one for that little stunt." His gaze held her still. "So you forgive me? Just like that?"

Feeling freer than she had in years, Tanya nodded and pointed a finger into his overwhelmingly gorgeous face. "If you ever hurt me again, I will never forgive you. Ever, Astacio. Do you hear me?"

"Loud and clear."

"Good." His alluring scent had her fighting the temptation to ask if they should kiss on it. She plowed forward with the business she'd been brought there to discus. "Now, about the interest. It stands."

"We'll see," he said. She bristled at that, her own favorite term for replacing *no way in hell will it happen*.

Ignoring his smirk, she went on with her list. "You mentioned changing the name. I have the final decision."

"It's your club and the name will also affect the restaurant, but I reserve the right to veto if it stinks," he said with a wrinkled nose.

She laughed. "You're horrible. About your birthday party—"

"Nonnegotiable." He shot out of his seat and glared down at her. "My thirtieth birthday party will be held there. After the changes we make, once people hit the spot, they'll never want to go anywhere else. I'm inviting everyone I know. It's going to be epic. I've already gotten in contact with Kiwi." He smirked at her gasp. "Not only did she say she'll come, but she'll sing."

She stood and placed her hands on her hips. "And Josh says *I'm* stubborn. You have it all over me, buddy. If you'd let me finish speaking, you would've heard me say that I need a party planner to get it done."

"Oh."

The sheepish expression tugged at her heart and she took a step away from him instead of forward. "You're a star in your own right, and neither I nor Clint know how to prepare for an event that big. And while we're at it, Mr. Big Shot, since you're going to be drawing in such a huge crowd, I think we should hire an in-house event planner."

He stared at her for a moment and then, without warning, he swooped down and wrapped his arms around her, swinging her in a circle while laughing.

Placing her on her feet after his moment of mania passed, dizziness made her stumble and she braced her hands on his chest to avoid a fall.

"I've missed you so much." He tucked her hair behind her ears while all she could do was stare up at him with what she hoped wasn't adoration blazing from her eyes. "I will never, ever hurt you again. You have my word." The soft brush of his lips against her forehead drew her closer to the point of wanting to stay in his embrace forever.

Self-preservation reared its logical head and she pushed away from him. She'd accepted his friendship, but anything more would end up in disaster, considering their social backgrounds.

She smoothed a hand over her skirt. "Do you have any ideas for event planners?"

"I'll have Toshia plan my birthday party. She'd kill me if I didn't. And she's the best in the business. I'll ask Lanelle if she can recommend someone for the club. She's always organizing fund-raisers. By the way, I need your accounts so she can go through them."

Tanya shook her head, happy to be back on a course she was more familiar with. Antagonizing him had always been so much fun. "Okay, but it would've been considerate if you'd talked to me about it before her." And with that, they were back in their groove. Friends once again. If only her treacherous emotions weren't pushing for more.

Chapter 11

Standing with her hands braced on her full hips, Tanya was a sight Miguel couldn't believe he'd gotten a second chance to be near again. Together on the third floor of the empty club, they perused the place in an attempt to have her see his vision. If they weren't on such a tight schedule, he'd savor their little fights more. He was ecstatic to be with her even if it was the crack of dawn on a Sunday morning so they could attempt to strategize.

The fact that she'd forgiven him so readily said a lot about her character, and he was grateful. They'd spent the past week coming up with a structural plan for the club. Or at least they'd tried to.

Their ideas tended to verge off into opposite directions instead of flowing into one. How many arguments had they had as they met either at her office or his? Nothing had gotten their joint stamp of approval. Had he been wrong to think they'd be able to work together to make this club a success?

One thing he knew for certain was that being around her kept him in a state of constant arousal and he desired her. The more time they spent together, the more he realized her beauty, strength, courage, kindness and caring nature fit him perfectly. And yet she remained completely out of his reach.

Maintaining their renewed friendship was most important. Soon she'd learn that they'd make an excellent couple. That's if his lifestyle didn't scare her away first. She'd made more than one comment over the past week about how he'd lived these past years, especially about his love for the opulence he'd become accustomed to.

Who didn't want suits that fit like a second skin, meals that caused him to have tiny orgasms with each bite and cars that showcased his personality? He enjoyed his lifestyle and couldn't see himself giving it up.

She was the only woman who had never asked him for anything. Very unusual for someone who knew how much he liked to spend his money.

And he couldn't forget the paparazzi. The more he hung out with her, the closer they came to being discovered, even with his disguises. The term *only friends* meant nothing to the hawks. They'd spin it into a tale worth selling, and he feared she'd cut things off when she learned just how vicious they could be when they were on the hunt for gossip.

Josh's friendship factored in, too. His best friend was a treasure he didn't know how to give up. He'd been seeking a way to ask for permission to attempt to date his sister. Everything he came up with just sounded wrong.

He'd figure something out, but right now he had to deal with Tanya's indecisiveness about her club. "Do you know what you want?"

She scrubbed her hands down her face and pouted at him. "Another scone, but you finished off the last one."

He chuckled. Damn, she knew how to entertain him. "You know what I mean. Can you envisage the club?"

Her shoulders slumped with her deep sigh. "To be honest, no."

Her defeated stance hurt him enough to sling an arm over her shoulder and draw her into his side. For once, she didn't move away, but lay her head against him. "Then why have you been fighting every decision instead of trusting my vision?"

He waited for her to answer. Silence. As much as he hated releasing her, he turned her toward him. Keeping his hands braced on her shoulders, he witnessed the misery lurking in her eyes. "What's wrong, baby?"

Her eyes sparked up at him for a moment. Did she like it when he called her what he wanted instead of being proper? She'd never mentioned it before, so he kept doing it. It just felt right.

More concerned about her than the club, he squeezed her shoulders when she didn't speak. "Talk to me."

"Today would've been our three-year anniversary."

Her delivering a haymaker to his jaw couldn't have surprised him more. His heart sank to the floor. How could he have forgotten? He'd been trying to find ways to get them together when she'd been mourning the loss of a marriage.

He led her to a chair and pulled it out. "Do you need a drink? It's—" he flipped his watch over "—eight o'clock in the morning, but a mimosa won't hurt. I'll look the other way if you want rum."

A crooked smile brightened her face, tugging at his heart. He should always be the one to make her happy. "Want to talk about it?" He remembered how she'd crumpled in his arms when she'd mentioned her ex-husband during their first meeting. If she ever loved him half as much as she had Broderick, he'd thank his lucky stars and hold on to her forever.

She loved you once, and you threw it back in her face. Never again, he promised. He'd cherish her to his dying breath if she'd have him. First, he had to help her get over her ex. To do that, he needed to be a true friend and listen, even if it hurt like he'd been pistol-whipped to hear that she was still in love with her ex.

As low as she felt at the moment, Miguel had amazed her. Did she want to talk about it? Listening to her rant about her loveless marriage wasn't his purpose in her life. They were supposed to be figuring out how to make her club a success, which she wasn't helping with by fighting him at every turn. Why? Was she trying to sabotage her life by prolonging the renovations so they wouldn't meet the deadline?

More like she just couldn't visualize the changes he wanted to make. Was the extra expense necessary? Wouldn't his birthday celebration being held there be enough to increase the patronage of the club? It would help if he didn't slam every idea she came up with for the club's name. "Club Venus" got an eye roll. "The Dance Den" had him laughing for a full minute. Thinking about the cages he'd suggested, she'd come up with "The Cage," which just got ignored. She had to admit she'd pitched some inappropriate names. She was looking for something that would show she'd risen above the pain and heartache thrown her way. Maybe personalizing the club wasn't the best idea.

"C'mon," he said encouragingly. "You know I'm a good listener. Get what's bothering you off your chest."

No second invitation needed. "Did you know we met the night…" She glanced away as the ache returned. She'd forgiven Miguel, so she had no right to feel anything about what he'd done to her that night. *Good luck.* She forced a smile. "We had that, um, difference of opinion."

His expression remained neutral, but he didn't correct her.

"I was so upset, I literally ran into Broderick." She ignored the sudden twitch of Miguel's jaw that she noted every time she mentioned her ex. Was he jealous? "You know how huge he is. When I was the one to stumble back instead of him, it took me by surprise. And when he was kind enough to ask what was wrong, it all spilled out. That's how our friendship started."

"Because of me." His voice sounded gruff.

She'd cursed Miguel a thousand times since then, wondering just how different her life might have been if he'd made a different choice. "Yes. When he proposed years later, I jumped at the opportunity. The guys weren't knocking down the door of an overweight workaholic."

"Workaholic?"

She reached out to smooth his raised eyebrow, thought better of it and placed her hand on the table. Why was it so difficult to keep her body parts to herself while around him? "I told you about my full-time computer-programming job and working in the restaurant. I made loads of money, but never had time to date. Or maybe it was the lack of men wanting to date me. Either way, when Broderick asked, I said yes."

He didn't meet her gaze when he asked, "Did you love him?"

How much should she share? "I did. Very much."

His Adam's apple bobbed before he said, "Oh." Was he upset or surprised that she could fall in love with someone else?

"We were great friends. Got along well and agreed about almost everything." Passion had never been in the cards for them. At first, she'd thought it was because she'd been overweight, but when she'd slimmed down, the sex still seemed perfunctory. She'd presumed she just wasn't made to have good sex. If she'd known Broderick was in the closet, she wouldn't have taken all the blame.

She placed her arms across her chest as the memories tumbled over each other. "He was an ideal husband. I'm talking flowers and gifts when I least expected them, and he took care of me as if I were the most precious thing in the world to him. It was like he was always coming up with ways to make sure I knew he appreciated me and enjoyed being married to me." She shook her head at the regret of being spoiled so lavishly and then losing it even though they'd both known something was missing in their on-paper perfect marriage. "Unfortunately, I never fell in love with him." *My heart always belonged to you and never let me forget it.*

His shoulders relaxed and his eyes twinkled with a repressed grin. "So your heart wasn't breaking a few minutes ago when you looked as if someone had stolen your favorite Ohio State sweatshirt."

She smiled at the shared memory. "I never forgave you for scaring me half to death. I loved that top."

He chuckled, and the misery that had filled her a moment ago dissipated. "You wore it all the time. You needed an intervention."

"Not even Josh was so mean as to sneak into my room and take it."

"Maybe he didn't care enough."

When had the club turned into a sauna? Water would be perfect to quench her suddenly dry mouth. Had he really cared about her back then? Everything in her bones had told her he had, but it had all gone downhill after she'd made the mistake of initiating that fateful, magnificent kiss. She'd loved him so much, and holding back for a moment longer may have broken her heart even more than expressing it had.

"If you aren't heartbroken over Broderick—" there was that little snarl again "—then what's wrong?"

Tapping her fingers in a tuneless beat on the surface of the table she tried to articulate the issue. She'd been antsy and indecisive all week, not just with Miguel when they'd met twice to discuss the club. "It's… I don't know."

Miguel reached out and covered her hyperactive hands. His comforting warmth seeped into her and she struggled to keep from turning her hands over so they could be palm to palm.

"I know you might end up beating me senseless for saying this, but take it easy."

"I've made some really bad mistakes." Her gaze gravitated to his protective hand over hers and she realized it wouldn't last so there was no need to even have it now. She slid her hand from beneath his and hugged herself. Grabbing her sides at his look of disappointment kept her from placing her fingers back into his strong comforting grasp.

"We all have," he said. "It's part of life's learning process."

"I'm having difficulty trusting that I'll make the right decisions, so I must've subconsciously decided to make none." She opened her arms out wide. "This is a lot of responsibility. What if I fail like Broderick said I would?"

He clenched his hand into a fist. "We weren't tight in college, but the more I hear about him, the more I want to crush him."

How did one respond to such vehemence? Not by smiling, that's for sure. Chastising him would be appropriate, but the happiness won out and she covered her mouth to hide it. "He wasn't a bad guy, just pissed that he had to give up his precious club by a court order once he'd decided to follow his bliss. He treated me really well while we were married. One time—"

He stood with enough force to rock the chair. "I don't need to hear your feel-good stories about him." He took a few steps toward the bar before returning to his seat. "How can I help you boost your confidence?

Since it's my fault you ended up in this situation in the first place, I'd like to make things right."

Had he really just said that? "You're not responsible for my bad decisions. Yes, what happened between us influenced my life, but I had a choice. Always. So please don't feel guilty about my current state of instability. It's all on me."

She wiggled in her seat when all he did was stare at her. "What?"

"You're an amazing woman."

Touched, she whispered, "Thank you."

The intimate moment was broken when he clapped his hands once. "I have an idea."

His enthusiasm startled her. "Shoot, Mr. Astacio. The floor is yours." She swung her arm in a wide arc. "Literally."

"Ha-ha. I have a feeling you never really did the club scene."

"Don't start. Who had to maintain her 3.7 GPA even though you tried to destroy it by always ragging on me about studying too much?"

"And who—" he pointed finger guns in her direction "—ended up tossing away her degree to run a nightclub? That's ironic."

"Don't ya think?" They said it at the same time and laughed. They used to have so much fun making up lyrics to the old Alanis Morissette song. It turned out that irony was more difficult to sing about than they'd initially thought.

Why couldn't the whole day go on like this? She'd missed how things used to be with them. Light and easy. Now she had it back. *For how long?* It didn't matter. Friendship had no expiration date. But a niggling fear settled behind her breastbone. What if she fell in love with him again? The way things were going, she'd fail a polygraph no matter what answer she gave, because she'd never stopped.

Tanya waited for the dread to settle in. Nothing came. As much as she should run away as if her addiction to carbs had returned, she knew this time nothing would develop from her feelings. He'd be her friend, and that was all. It would hurt to see him date other women. Even the thought brought a haze of green to her vision. She'd always hated how jealous she'd gotten when he hung out with the beautiful women who chased him on campus. She never impugned them, though. If she had looked like she did today, she'd have done the same as them.

Liar. She'd wanted more. A commitment. His whole heart focused on her. She doubted he could ever provide it to her. Or any woman. His free-spirited, fun-loving, passion-seeking personality wouldn't allow it, so she shouldn't expect it of him. She'd never get it.

Fully sober, she asked, "What's your point?"

"Gurl…" The word went on forever before his head started moving side to side with a finger waggle and he added a higher pitch to his voice. "You need to dip your toes into some red nail polish. Tease yo' hair, add a lot more makeup to your already stunning face and go club hopping to see what's out there." She would've been able to keep in her laughter at his overly effeminate gestures and speech, but the head toss and hair pat was too much to keep her straight-faced.

"I'm sure you remember that my husband left me for another man, yet you decide to play it gay?"

"Anything to make you laugh."

What was she going to do with him? "Thanks. So you want to go clubbing?"

"You need the exposure so you can experience my vision. By the time we finish our two-night tour, you'll be ready to tell me what this place needs."

She shook her head. "No way. Tanya needs her sleep. I'll do one night with you."

The gleam in those hazel eyes didn't bode well for her negotiation tactic. "That's what the days are for. You won't regret it. Two nights of partying will add more spice to your life. Pep to your step and groove to your move." He did the last with a full body roll. "Guaranteed."

"Nice commercial." What would it be like to go out and just have fun with him? Being together for two days straight appealed most. It didn't matter what they were doing—his presence had both a calming and exciting effect on her that she couldn't get enough of. "Fine. No need to get any more dramatic about it. I'll go." *And risk losing even more of my heart to you.*

Chapter 12

Tanya had a way of taking everything Miguel knew about himself and throwing it out the window, making him see the truth. Never had he been more real with someone than with her. That's what she requested from him, so he readily gave it. She'd captured him just by allowing him to be himself.

His mother had often bragged that from the moment he'd been born, females had flocked around him. As he grew, he'd learned when to flash his smile in a way that had them fanning themselves and giggling. He knew the power of his hazel eyes, dimples and thick curly hair, and used them to his advantage.

Charm and good looks didn't work with Tanya. Back in college, he hadn't wanted it to. He'd desired her to like him for who she got to know. Preserving his friendship with Josh had been an even bigger necessity. Now, as a grown man who'd changed over the years, he knew what he wanted. Yes, Josh's friendship still meant the world to him, but he needed Tanya in his life. She was what had been missing in all of those failed relationships, he just hadn't realized it. Until now.

Maybe it was their history of being real with each other. Or the fact that he'd been attracted to her from the first moment they'd met. Or even that fate had thrown her into his path. He didn't know the reason he loved her, only that he did.

"When you said we'd be going clubbing, I thought you meant in Cleveland." Tanya ran her hand over the wood paneling of his family's private jet. Now that they were airborne, the shock seemed to have worn off. "You sneaky man. That early dinner invitation was a good cover to get me here for the five o'clock takeoff."

He laughed, recalling her open mouth when he'd had his driver drop them off at the airport. He loved surprising her. Back in school, she wouldn't accept any of the expensive gifts he'd tried to give for her birthday or Christmas, but when he did something that pleased her, she accepted it. The difficult part had been figuring out what would make her happy. It took a lot of observation and listening on his part. Simple things like reminding her that her favorite show was on when she got lost in her studies would make her beam. Even though he'd hated the vampire-turned-good show with a white-hot passion, he'd sit and watch the whole thing with her just to be near her.

"You know I don't do things small. You need to

experience the hottest clubs so yours can be comparable."

"Ever heard of the internet? Lots of pictures and even videos." For a moment, a vise gripped his chest as her tone rose. Was she upset with him? And then she kicked her feet in the air and squealed. "I'm just playing. Now that my little lecture is over, thank you so much, Miguel. I can't believe I'm actually on a private plane." She sucked in her cheeks and posed. "I feel like a movie star. Now I can say I've jet-setted."

The lit-up seat belt sign was the only thing stopping him from scooping her into his arms and squeezing her close. Her joy was his, and he loved the challenge of figuring out what made her happy. "That's not a word."

"Who cares? It's what I am now." Her glittery dark eyes gazed into his, and her smile did things to his body only she could relieve. "Now that you've kidnapped—"

"I did no such thing. You sprinted onto the plane, not caring if I was with you or not."

Her giggle tickled him. "I love to travel."

He remembered. It didn't matter where, either. When he'd talked about all the places he'd been, she'd sighed in longing and told him about the family vacations they'd taken when she was younger. "Sometimes I wonder if I'll ever have time to enjoy life like I did when I was a child," she'd once said after telling him about one of her trips.

He had vowed that day to show her the world. And then he'd messed it all up and lost her. Now that he'd gotten a second chance, at least at her friendship, he'd make sure to fulfil his promise.

"Where are we going?"

"New York City."

She clasped her hands under her chin. "Oh, my goodness. You are just too damn much." And then she frowned. "I didn't bring clothes for an overnight trip."

He scanned her conservative black suit skirt with the sparkly blouse, which she'd topped off with a jacket. "You did understand when I told you we were going clubbing, right?"

She looked down at her clothes with her arms spread open. "I look fine."

"Sure, if you're going to work for an accounting firm. Before we hit the clubs, we're going shopping. Don't worry about the things you'll need for overnight—it's on me."

"You will not buy me clothes, Astacio." She squinted her eyes and raised her voice to a near roar. "Do you hear me?"

He pretended to clean out his ears. "I think the pilot heard you. Can you honestly tell me that you're dressed to party in the most popular nightclubs in New York?"

The apparent war occurring in her analytical mind raged for a few seconds before she relented. "No. But if you'd told me where we were going, I could've prepared better."

He snorted. "I doubt it. Every time I see you, you're wearing something similar. Do you own clothes that show off your fabulous body? You worked hard for it—let the world see it."

"I'm not dressing like a hoochie."

He burst out laughing and couldn't stop. His ribs hurt.

The pilot turned off the seat belt sign. She unclicked her belt and angled her body toward him. "I mean it. I'll pay for my own clothes. I may not be in the same class as you, but I'm not poor."

His lingering smile left. Where had that come from? Most women liked that he was willing to lavish gifts on them. Once again, Tanya proved to be the absolute opposite. "No one said you were. What was that crack about not being in my class?"

She turned to the window where they flew among the clouds. "Never mind."

"That's not the way we roll. Tell me what's bothering you."

"You're rich."

He waited for the problem. "And…"

"I'm not. The two can't hang out together. Back in college, you lived in a dorm room, ate in the cafeteria and made friends with the locals." She waved her arms around the cabin's luxurious space. "This isn't the guy I knew back then."

"I hate to burst your bubble, but I've always been wealthy. Have you forgotten those rides I used to give you in my Aston Martin?" He tried really hard to figure out what was going on in her mind. "What's this about?"

Her shoulders slumped with her heavy sigh. "Our friendship is unbalanced. There's nothing I can offer you that you don't have. Even now, you're doing everything to help me get my club back on its feet and I can't even pay you."

Yet another novel position she'd put him in. "We may not be financially equal, but you're greater than me in so many ways that I envy you. Just by being your amazing self, you make me feel special. You treat me like a person, not a money machine. That respect is what makes us equal."

"Oh."

"Is that all you have to say?"

She shrugged with an exaggerated "Meh."

Tears rolled down his eyes with the laughter she'd evoked. He would never get tired of being with her. If he had his way, he'd make sure she realized just how good they could be together. Not just good, but perfect.

Chapter 13

Tanya could get used to Miguel's lifestyle. The room at the Worthington Hotel in Manhattan was by far the most lavish she'd ever been in. Carpet so thick she feared tripping, a four-poster bed she had to climb a step to get into and, if she could pretend to be pregnant with the thick duvet tucked under her clothes, she'd steal it. The gourmet dinner they'd eaten at the restaurant had been divine.

She'd be destitute if things didn't improve with the club, but she'd ended up in one of the most luxurious hotels in New York, all because Miguel had apologized and she'd forgiven him for his past transgression. It hadn't been difficult because she'd missed him so much over the years.

His speech about how much he respected her and considered her his equal had spread a lovely warmth through her whole body. She'd been ready to crawl into his lap, entrap his cheeks between her hands and meld their lips together until they were both groaning. She'd distracted herself from falling into the urge just in time. Making the same mistake twice in a lifetime would discredit her hard-earned wisdom.

Their lifestyles were mismatched, but at least he knew she wasn't using him for his money. She'd rather go back to her heaviest weight without the deliciousness of the binge eating than for him to think it was a remote possibility.

After ten minutes of gazing out the window at the perfect nighttime skyline of the Big Apple, a knock sounded at the door. Tanya went to the intricately carved panel and looked through the peephole. A petite Asian woman about her age stood on the other side with a clothes rack. "Good evening, Ms. Carrington. My name is Mei Ito from Saks Fifth Avenue. Mr. Coleman arranged to have you try on some dresses for your outings tonight and tomorrow."

Mr. Coleman? Her brain raced through the Rolodex of her mind to find anyone she knew by that name, and then it hit her. Miguel was playing secret agent again. So he wouldn't even let her go out to shop, which meant she couldn't purchase her own clothes. The crafty scoundrel.

Tanya stepped out the way after opening the door so Mei could roll the clothes in. She stretched out an arm with a lavender overnight bag in her hand. "This is for you, too. All the things you'll need to sleep comfortably tonight, including slippers."

Her heart melted. Miguel had thought of everything. Then something in her hardened as if the molten lava of her organs had been splashed with arctic water. He was a ladies' man. Of course he knew just what a woman needed in an overnight case. She wondered if he had a bunch of them hidden in the plane so he'd always be ready.

"Mr. Coleman has a good eye." Mei slid a hanger to the left of the rack. "He told me to bring most of the clothes in a size twelve."

How had he known? It had taken a year of sheer willpower and exercise, despite Broderick's discouragement, to shrink from a size twenty-four to a twelve. She wasn't as skinny as she'd thought she'd be at the beginning of the process, but she was happy with her health. It might take more time to get accustomed to looking into a mirror and seeing the woman with the curvaceous figure staring back at her. Sometimes she still felt as if she were obese.

Mei pulled out a brightly patterned blue, green, red and white Lycra jumpsuit that dipped too low in the back for Tanya's comfort. She waved her hands in front of her to keep the revealing outfit away. All of her lumps and bumps would show if she struggled into it. "Do you have anything a little looser?"

"With your curves, it would look spectacular, but if you aren't comfortable, then try this one." She pulled another dress off the line and handed it over.

An electric-blue sheath dress made out of the softest silk she'd ever touched. The sleeves billowed out past her elbows and the hemline hit just at the knee. Before she could turn to skip into the bathroom, Mei pulled out a bag from the lower shelf of the rack. "He wasn't as sure about your lingerie size, so there are various ones in here for you to choose from. He said to remind you to take as many as you want."

She drew the line at him buying her underwear, but taking it out on the woman wouldn't be appropriate. She'd save her annoyance for Miguel. With the satchel in hand, she headed to the bathroom.

Ignoring the bag was impossible, so she hung the gorgeous dress on the door and unzipped it. The most beautiful bras and panties assaulted her eyes, and she groaned. The temptation to take all of them, whether they fit or not, hit her hard. She pulled out a stunning deep-purple-and-turquoise number and checked the tag. Thirty-six C. Perfect. After slipping off her own clothes, she tried on the bra. Her breasts sat up as if begging for someone to reach out and grab them, and talk about comfortable. She shimmied her shoulders and found it supported her.

Damn, Miguel. She shouldn't want to keep it, but she wouldn't fight with herself, especially over something so beautiful. Digging into the bag, she found the matching panties in her size, happy to see they were high cut rather than a thong.

Weren't they partying for two nights? Maybe another set would be in order. And she had to get home on Sunday. Three in total, and that would be the end. No more gifts from Miguel for the rest of her life. The canary-yellow-and-tan-lace concoction beckoned to her along with an emerald green satin one. Both fit her like a dream.

After releasing the dress from its hanger, she slid it over her body. She hoped the moan at being swathed in something that had to be as soft as an angel's wings didn't carry out of the massive bathroom to where Mei could hear. The material was so luxurious it brought tears to her eyes. She stood up straight at the sight of herself in the mirror. Was this hot woman her?

She turned and so did the lady in the mirror. She smiled at her reflection. For the first time in her life, she fell in love with herself. No longer did the woman with low self-esteem about her body shine through her eyes. She'd taken the knocks life had thrown her way and grown into someone more beautiful because of them.

Grabbing the new goodies, she stepped out of the bathroom with her head held high.

"You look outstanding," Mei said before pulling out a dusky-pink leather skirt paired with a gold off-the-shoulder long-sleeved thin sweater. The last ensemble consisted of a more casual pair of ash-colored wool trousers and an exquisite violet blouse. Tanya's head nodded in agreement at Mei's very professional eye before taking them to try on.

The garments were perfect. She slid the electric-blue dress back on and sighed with bliss before heading out. "They're both wonderful," she said, still gazing at the leather skirt she would dance the hell out of tomorrow night.

"You are a vision." The deep Southern-accented voice that sent a tingle from her head down to her big toe didn't belong to Mei.

Her mind went blank when she beheld the man standing before her. Miguel had changed and tried to hide his appearance, but she saw straight through the disguise. The artistic makeup altered the angle of his eyes. She didn't know how he'd done it, but his nose appeared wider and the fake full beard seemed real. Just like the first time they'd met at her club, he'd darkened his skin, but the stomach paunch was new. Once again, the dark brown contact lenses disturbed her. Dressed in a dark, rather plain and unflattering suit with a dark blue shirt underneath, she wouldn't have given him a second glance if she saw him on the street.

She grinned. If his goal was not to be noticed in a crowd where everyone tried to look their best, then he'd done a brilliant job. "Thank you. You look, um, good, too."

He angled his head, which was covered by a short Afro wig, toward her.

Mei held out a stunning beige pair of low-slung, open-toed, kitten-heeled shoes. "Please try these on."

With a quick look at Miguel, she reached for the shoes feeling like Cinderella. Glad she'd done her nails last weekend, the pink polish of her toes peeked through as she slipped her foot in. Once again, a fantastic fit. Mei smiled at her and pulled out one more pair for her to try on. This one was a simple black pump with a wedge heel.

Was it a coincidence or had he remembered that her lower back didn't do well with high heels? Even after she'd lost the weight, they were still torture devices. "You have wonderful taste, Mei. Thank you for bringing over such beautiful clothes."

The petit woman laughed with a head toss, flipping her hair over her shoulder. "I can't take the credit. Mr. Coleman asked me to grab the clothes from the Astacio line, Entonne."

Tanya's brow curved upward so high she thought it touched her hairline. She was wearing the clothing line his family had created. They didn't cater to middle-class folks, so she knew the clothes she'd be wearing over the weekend would put her credit card in the red. "Thank you for coming to dress me."

"It's always a pleasure to see lovely clothes on such a beautiful woman."

Miguel stepped forward and claimed Tanya's hand. The soft brush of his lips against her knuckles sent electricity bursting up her arm. "I couldn't have said it better myself."

Too enthralled with the web of sensuality he'd encased them in, Tanya barely noticed as Mei bade them goodbye and pushed the rack out the door.

Suddenly shy, she looked up at him through her lashes. "Thank you for the clothes. They're gorgeous."

"Not even half as stunning as you. I can't wait to show you off tonight."

For the first time in her life, she couldn't wait to be seen. Being Cinderella wouldn't be a bad thing. Not if she could pretend, if only for the weekend, that Miguel were her prince.

Chapter 14

"Where did Mr. Coleman come from?" Tanya asked as the limo took them to their destination.

Miguel had known she wouldn't be able to stop herself from asking. She hadn't inquired about the costume she'd seen him wear to her club. He blamed it on the shock she must've had with the changes he'd recommended.

He found it impossible to look away from her glamorous beauty. He'd had a makeup-and-hair stylist drop by to do something quick. He'd warned them not to use a heavy hand because she didn't need it. What they'd done to her made her glow as her updo emphasized her oval face, high cheekbones and full lips.

All he wanted to do was kiss those glossy lips. Did they taste as sweet and succulent as the raspberries they reminded him of?

The snapping of fingers in his face brought him back. "Earth to Mr. Coleman."

He reached forward for his glass of champagne to wet his desert of a mouth and stall for time. Maybe she'd forget her question.

Tanya waved her hand from his realistic-looking wig down to his non-designer-shoe-covered feet. "What's up with this look?"

"Does it bother you?" Unable to resist, he slid his finger along the smooth curve of her neck and enjoyed her shudder at his touch before she swatted his hand away. He smiled, expecting nothing less. He wouldn't have minded if she'd grabbed his hand and kissed his palm, but they weren't at that point yet. "Would you like me to show a little more skin?"

She sucked her teeth and rolled her eyes. "Tell me."

Her lips tipping downward worried him. Why did she think he was dressed up like this? "I don't want to be recognized."

She nodded and her mouth dipped farther downward, but she didn't say anything else.

"What's wrong?"

"You seem to wear disguises when you're with me. Are you embarrassed to be seen with me? I know I used to be bigger and I still haven't lost—"

"No. Not at all." For her to think he didn't want to be seen with her hurt. How could she think such a thing? He grabbed her hand and kissed the knuckles. She took in a sharp breath, but didn't pull her hand out of his. "I have never been embarrassed to be seen with you. Not back in college, and certainly not now."

She stared at him as if trying to decipher the truth in his expression. Entranced, he rubbed slow circles on the back of her hand with his thumb. He could stay with her like this all night. He'd rather they be alone than share her with the club goers they were about to have a meaningless experience with.

He'd never felt this strong need to be with a woman before. Growing up was a fascinating experience.

"Then why the costumes?" she asked softly.

The limo stopped in front of a place where he could feel the music pumping even from inside the vehicle. Rather than get out, he pressed the intercom button and told the driver to make a ten-minute loop around the block. He had to explain to her the need for the disguises before the night went any further.

The woman he loved would never again feel insecure about something he'd done.

Miguel angled himself so his shoulder rested against the backrest, and he propped his knee on the seat. Her dark eyes implored him for an answer.

"It's no secret I used to be a wild young man."

Her snort eased the tension. "Used to be?"

"Yes. That's what this disguise is all about. If you've been following me in the entertainment sector, you'll have noticed that for the last six months I've maintained a pretty low profile." Had she been paying attention to his excursions? Her unchanged expression didn't give him a clue. He'd been on a binge of parties and women just to forget her. It never happened. She'd hovered.

"I still like to go out every once in a while, but it's no longer necessary for the media to always know about it."

"Why not?"

"Everyone must grow up at some point, right?"

Her pursed lips didn't denote belief in his words. "I'm vying for the position of Executive Public Relations Officer for Astacio Enterprises. The person currently in the position will be retiring next month."

Tanya nodded but her eyebrows remained crinkled.

"When my father offered me the job, he attached a single caveat."

"Stop all the partying and be a respectable member of society," she filled in.

He chuckled. "You said it as if you were in the room with us. At first, I threw a fit at his offer. He'd always tried to tone down my behavior with threats and promises. In the end, I did what I wanted and loved it." He leaned his head against the seat. "Other than your brother and my siblings, my parents know me better than anyone else in the world. They must've seen that I needed a change, but didn't know how to get me out of the lifestyle I'd entrapped myself in. When he gave me time to think about it, I did. I realized that my life had no purpose. No meaning. Jumping from party to party wasn't enough. Sure, I'd become the king of marketing, but there was still something missing." *You.*

All it had taken was her walking into his office that first day to realize how much he'd missed by not having her in his life. "Not that I thought speaking to the media about the state of the Astacio empire would bring meaning into my life, but I had to give it a try. So I accepted my father's challenge. He gave me until my thirtieth birthday. Six months to keep my name out of the headlines in any kind of way that wouldn't benefit the family or the company, and the job would be mine."

The past six months had been easier than he'd anticipated. The party lifestyle on an every-weekend basis no longer appealed to him. "Fund-raisers replaced partying all night with musicians, actors and pro athletes. I started spending more time at home and getting to know my family and found that I really liked them." He smiled. "You'll love my parents. And Lanelle is one of the sweetest people you'll ever meet. My older brother, Leonardo, can be boorish, but he means well."

She returned his grin. "Your hard-as-nails corporate-lawyer brother? What did the last article I read call him?" Tapping her chin, she thought for a second. "A ruthless barracuda."

Miguel laughed. "Yeah, he'll go for the jugular, especially when it comes to work, but he always has my back. Changing my life was one of the best things I've ever done."

He drew in her sweet scent as she reached out and rubbed her hand along his cheek. Moving might scare her away and there was nothing quite so exquisite as having her soft hand touch him.

"This is why tonight I'm out with a rather plain, slightly padded, bearded man," she said in a low voice when she removed her hand.

"Yeah. Plus I like dressing up. Being someone other than myself can be fun."

"But you're such a wonderful man."

He watched her, looking for any sign of sarcasm. His heart sped up and joy seeped into him when he found none. Did she think so? "I don't remember you having that opinion a few days ago."

Her eyes glimmered. "I've always thought so. Even when you acted like a punk."

"I was pretty good at it, wasn't I?"

"Sometimes too good. But, underneath, you were always a sweet guy and a true friend."

His head would explode soon, but then the reality of his life came crashing down. "There's another reason for the costume."

She arched a brow.

"The media can be relentless. If they saw us together, they'd come out with all sorts of rumors." He gazed into her eyes. "I want to protect you from all of that. If you aren't accustomed to the limelight, it can be daunting."

She looked away with a nod. "I understand."

He hooked a finger under her chin to have her look at him. "If it were up to me, I'd show you off to the world. You're the finest woman I've ever known, Tanya. You always have been." Just as he was about to lean in to kiss her, to finally indulge in the sweetness and passion he remembered, the car came to a stop.

She cleared her throat and glanced down at her watch. "It's already eleven. You said we have five hot spots to get to before the break of dawn. We'd better get started."

"Who's turned into the party girl?"

She raised her hands and shimmied her shoulders. "Me. Me."

He laughed and tapped on the glass divider so the chauffer could let them out. Yes, this was a business outing, but who was to say he couldn't show her the best time of her life? Maybe then he'd be able to work his way back into her heart.

Chapter 15

Miguel must have hundreds of layers to him, and Tanya was compelled to peel them all away to find out what goodness lay beyond each of the previous ones. *Why was she so fascinated with him?* The question had to wait for an answer because the hot song that pulsed into her had her dancing as they were whisked into Vespar.

He'd had the foresight to get his alias's name on the VIP list at the clubs so they had no difficulty getting in. They'd been escorted straight into the building and up the stairs to the VIP lounge. The music shook the walls as she bounced her upper body to the well-mixed beat.

If her club could be this trendy and packed, she'd own Cleveland. She slid closer to Miguel on the plush dark couch he'd chosen. "This place is amazing. Now I know what you mean about the dance cages." A couple danced in an elevated enclosure in the far corner of the club and seemed to be having the time of their lives. "But ours will be ground level. Less heart palpitations for me. The insurance premium must be crazy."

"I'm glad you're coming around to seeing things my way. What would you like to drink?" Miguel asked when the server sauntered over.

"A Long Island Iced Tea."

His brows rose to above the level of the ostentatious rose-tinted shades, but he didn't comment on her choice before turning his attention to the waitress. "One Long Island Iced Tea and a bottle of sparkling water."

The woman nodded and her smile widened as she said, "Anything you want." Even in this gruff disguise, Miguel's raw masculinity shone through.

He angled his body toward Tanya. "How the hell have things become such opposites in our relationship?"

She gave her hair a nervous pat, wishing she had the strong mixed drink in front of her now. *Relationship* was a broad term. They weren't dating. They were in business together. That's all. "Are you telling me you don't drink?"

"I do, but as I mentioned before, a lot has changed and my drinking habits are one of them. Now I stay sober when I'm partying. I see the truth of my circumstances." He shook his head. "No more imagined fun."

He slid the glasses down and pierced her with his dark gaze, making her wish she could remove the contact lenses to enjoy the uniqueness of his eyes. "But you never used to drink. Not even wine coolers."

She hitched a shoulder. "Broderick was a social

man. When we used to go out, he knew me well enough to order drinks I'd like. He was right every time."

His jaw muscle flexed, making the fake beard move. Bringing up her ex seemed to annoy him. Was he jealous? *Don't be silly. I'm simple little ol' me and he's the great Miguel Astacio.* They were worlds apart and the chasm was too wide to fill. She'd do well to remember that.

The server returned with their drinks and a wink for Miguel. Tanya's hand balled into a fist to punch the woman. With the coolness of her drink oozing into the pads of her fingers, she realized the absurdity of her reaction. Nobody had stolen Miguel's freedom or his healthy appetite for women, although she hadn't heard or read anything about him dating anyone in months. Maybe he'd gone out with his women while in disguise.

Or worse, they'd spent cozy evenings in his palatial home, laughing, talking and making love. She took a healthy swallow of her drink at the possibility of anyone but her laying a hand on him. The strength of the flavors danced on her tongue. It had to be one of the best she'd ever had. "It's good."

"And that's how a drink is supposed to be. While we're talking about drinks, you need to fire your manager."

Not this again. It had been a bone of contention between them every time they'd gotten together. Things really were all about business with him. For her, friendship and loyalty played a huge role. Clint had been both to her.

Another sip of the cocktail sent the familiar

warmth of alcohol sliding down her throat into her belly. "Have you heard back from your sister about the finances?"

"She said she'd have it to me sometime this week." What she could see of his face lit up and her skin heated without having to take a drink. "She said she would've had it done by now, but my niece is being a holy terror with her teething."

Nothing made her happier than experiencing the family side of him. "Poor thing. I've heard it can be bad."

"Chloe is normally such a calm baby." He pulled out his phone from his pocket and slid his finger over it until he found what he sought, then flung the phone in front of her. "Isn't she adorable?"

Were they really at one of the hottest clubs in New York City talking about babies? She reached out for the phone and became awed by the chubby cheeks. "She's beautiful. Look at all that curly hair, and those hazel eyes." Tanya grinned up at him. "Other than the dark skin, the girl is your little clone." She handed the phone back.

He glanced at the screen with a sappy grin. "She's my heart."

Tanya looked down at her body to make sure she hadn't actually melted. The man was killing her. Every moment, each revelation brought her closer to the fall. What was she talking about? She'd never gotten out of the deep pit of loving him. Only now, light seemed to be streaming in, making it a more comfortable place to be. This time she wouldn't do anything about it except to let him go when their time together was up. She pushed away the sad reminder. With one more long sip of her drink, she jumped up. "I don't know if your current persona dances, but I'm going to do some reconnaissance on that crowded floor."

His laughter as he stood pleased her. "If I let you out there alone looking as fine as you do, there's going to be a fight up in here."

"You're too much," she said, giggling before breezing away from him. The place was dark, but she was sure her skin radiated enough for him to see the flush of pleasure that had crept into her face. Yes, she was in big trouble.

Four in the morning and five clubs later, Miguel was ready to call it a night and cancel tomorrow evening's outing. Wouldn't it be nicer to spend the time with her in one of their hotel rooms and talk until the sun came up?

When had he changed so drastically? Back in the day, he would've taken a bunch of the club goers and moved the party to his place. Now all he wanted to do was escort this beautiful woman to his room and get lost in her. The image of her long, sexy limbs wrapped around him as he sank deep into her hadn't strayed far from his thoughts, keeping him in an uncomfortable semi-erect state all evening.

It hadn't helped when at the third club, she'd loosened up enough to grind up against him. His body had reacted. He knew she'd felt him, but she'd continued to undulate, driving him deeper into a state of need.

He shouldn't have let her have a drink at each club. The champagne had tipped her over the edge from tipsy to drunk, and he'd found her extremely entertaining. Even when inebriated, the woman had class—

only now whatever popped into her head came out with a limited filter.

They'd left the fourth club after fifteen minutes when Tanya had threatened a woman who'd tried to dance with him. He'd loved every minute of her jealousy. She still cared about him. Or was it just the alcohol making her possessive?

"I think this place is the bestest," Tanya slurred as she sank onto his lap in the armchair they'd occupied in the VIP section of Club Annex. She poked his cheek. "You are so right about the Ple…Plex…um, glass. We can see everyone and they can see us, but it still gives us privacy." She took off his sunglasses. "I hate these contact lenses." He caught her hand before she could go for his eye to remove the lens.

Would he ever get the chance to hold her like this again? Enjoy this uninhibited side of her?

She snatched her hand out of his and stroked his face. "You shouldn't hide your eyes under a bushel. They're too beautiful."

Her lush body against his and her soft fingers stroking his skin stole away any ability to think logically. "Bushel?"

Slapping his shoulder, she giggled. "Yeah, like in the good book when we're told not to hide our light under a bushel."

He laughed. "I get it. Are you ready to go?"

She stuck out her bottom lip, and it had taken extreme willpower not to pull it into his mouth, laving it with his tongue and applying a gentle suction.

"I'm not ready." She wiggled her hips in rhythm to the reggae tune playing. The exquisite torture was too much, so he lifted her onto the space next to him.

Gripping his arm, she gazed up at him. "You are so strong to be able to lift a hefty girl like me."

One thing he hadn't liked about her drunk personality was the disparaging remarks about herself. As if she didn't see herself in the new light she'd stepped into. She hadn't believed him when he'd countered them.

"Baby, I'll always be able to carry you." And he meant it in more than a physical way. He'd support her no matter what she was going through. He'd stand by her side. If she'd let him.

Getting up, he reached a hand down to her and she took it, sending a shock of electrical energy through him.

She swept her other arm toward the dance floor. "Let's boogie."

He laughed at her enthusiasm and couldn't bring himself to diminish it by telling her he wanted to go back to the hotel, so he found a space against the wall and watched his woman dance. He stepped away when anyone, man or woman, dared to try to get with her, but Tanya didn't seem to notice them. Her gaze held his throughout her slow, sensual dances.

He experienced an intense need for her. He'd ensure that the clubs they'd go to in Miami would only play fast music, even if he had to bribe the DJ to make it happen. There was no way he could go through this for another night without having an outlet other than a cold shower or self-gratification.

Seduction wasn't in his game plan when it came to Tanya. He wanted her to desire him as much as he did her. And to fall in love with him again. He had a lot of work to do to make it happen. Her generous spirit had forgiven him, but, unfortunately, she'd built up some kind of wall using their social standings as the bricks. He'd do his best to make sure she felt cherished, worthy and beautiful for the rest of her life.

Chapter 16

Tanya moaned as she snuggled into the warm body behind her. *Warm body?* Her eyes popped open only to slam shut against the brightness. She squinted to find herself in a strange room with an arm resting over her hip. She scrambled away from the body and held her hands up to defend herself.

A wide-awake, bare-chested Miguel lay on the other side of the bed, smiling. "Good morning. I was wondering when you'd wake up."

The sight of the man's glorious muscular body didn't do anything to stop her heart from trying to burst through her chest. Tearing her gaze from him, she glanced around the room. They were in her hotel suite. She looked down her body and saw her rumpled club clothes.

Her mouth felt fuzzy and plain nasty. "You forced

me to drink a whole bottle of water last night." Was that what she was going with? Asking why the hell she was in bed with him would've made a lot more sense.

He propped himself onto one of his defined arms, making her mouth go even dryer. "Do you have a headache?"

She did a self-assessment. "No." How much had she had to drink last night? Without warning, the memory of the best night of her life came flooding back. Mortified at her behavior, she scrambled off the bed and pointed in the direction of the bathroom. She backed away, keeping a close eye on him like any prey would do her predator. Only she'd been the one to attack him last night.

In the bathroom she gasped as she looked in the mirror. Makeup smeared, hair a wild mess—and was that dried saliva on her cheek? What had she been thinking when she'd asked him to spend the night with her?

That's why she rarely drank. It lowered her inhibitions so that her truest desires came to her without her having to think about it. She'd craved him last night. The bulge in his trousers as she'd ground against him had told her he'd wanted her, too.

And yet here she stood, fully clothed without a pulsing awareness between her legs that would've told her if they'd made love.

She emptied her bladder, brushed her teeth, scrubbed her face and smoothed down her hair as she struggled to remember what he'd said after she'd offered herself to him.

Taking a deep breath, she reached for the door to face the man who'd rejected her. Again. Her knees went weak when his words from last night hit her like a tempest. He'd held her by the shoulders as she'd struggled to get closer to kiss his tempting lips, to offer herself to him. "Don't get me wrong, I want you." His voice had been deep, husky. "So damn much I can't see straight, but you're drunk."

She'd protested with slurred words, but he'd ignored her. "When we make love, it'll be with a clear head. You'll feel and remember every touch and stroke we share, and you'll know who gave you pleasure beyond any you've experienced before. And then—" he'd brushed his lips against the shell of her ear, making her shiver "—you'll ask for more."

If he'd thought his words would cool her ardor, he'd been wrong and she'd tried to leap onto him. That's when he'd kissed her forehead and forced a bottle of water on her. By the time she'd finished drinking, fatigue had descended and when she lay down, her eyes closed. The last thing she remembered saying was, "Please don't leave me, Miguel."

The mattress had dipped behind her as he'd pressed his body against her back. "Never, baby. I'll never leave you again. And I promise not to do anything to make you want to go. It's you and me, my love. You and me."

With that she'd fallen asleep. Smiling.

Had he really said those sweet, tender words to her instead of taking her like she'd begged him to do? Had he really called her his love? Her throat tightened at the memory. But it didn't mean anything; it couldn't. He'd been using terms of endearment since the first day she'd stepped into his office. He must throw them out like Hollywood agents did to their clients.

She stepped into the room. Miguel still lay on her bed, looking good enough to make her want to fly into his arms. That wouldn't happen so she walked to the window and looked down at the ant-like people filling the street eighteen stories below. Why not keep things light and let the night fall away like the dream it had seemed to be. "What time is it?"

"Ten minutes to noon."

"Wow. I can't believe I slept so late."

"You had a good time last night." She jumped as his voice came from directly behind her, but she couldn't bear to face him. Not after the way she'd behaved. "Are you hungry? I ordered breakfast," he said.

The pangs of an empty belly hit her. "I could eat. Thanks for forcing that water down me last night."

"Tanya."

"Yes." She hated the shyness that had come over her. Couldn't she wind back the hands of time and make things between them comfortable again? She'd have to go back to before she'd ever laid eyes on him in college, and she never wanted to have never known him. Even after everything she'd been through, meeting him was the best thing to happen to her.

"Sweetheart, look at me."

The butterflies in her stomach took flight, but she feigned interest in the occurrences of the busy city. She had no choice but to obey when he grasped her shoulders and turned her. Staring at his chest did nothing to ease her anxiety, so she took a leap and looked up into his eyes. Back to the brilliant hazel she'd always loved.

For every moment they stood gazing at each other, she sank deeper. She could barely remember who she'd been when he hadn't been in her life for the past ten years. He was her world at that moment and nothing else mattered.

Her breaths came out in little pants as dread competed with nerve-racking anticipation. Would he kiss her? The air pulsed around them. Pushing her from behind to get closer and press her lips against his to see if what they'd shared all those years ago had been real. History stopped her from taking the plunge. If anything were to happen between them, he'd have to initiate. Not her.

He held her gaze as he lowered his head. If he feared she'd move away, he was mistaken. A knock on the door made them both jump. Miguel glowered in the direction of the offender. The person would be in deep trouble if he answered the door.

The incredible moment dissipated as quickly as it had arrived. She hitched a thumb toward the barrier, keeping the intruder safe from his wrath. "I'll get it."

Scrubbing both hands down his face, Miguel berated himself. He'd had his chance. Twice. Last night, she'd offered herself to him and he'd let the opportunity slide by. If only she'd been sober, he wouldn't have hesitated to finally show rather than tell her just how much he loved her. Had always loved her.

He'd been strong when her tantalizing full breasts had pressed up against his chest and she'd slurred that she wanted to make love to him. Her hot, alcohol-infused breath in his face wasn't a turn-on, but the fact that her inhibitions had lowered so she'd admitted she wanted him had him on an emotional high.

He'd spent the night cuddled with her when she'd

asked him to stay. Her soft, curvaceous body had enticed him, and he couldn't leave her. After what had seemed like hours, he'd finally fallen asleep to the sound of her soft snores.

"Good morning." The waiter rolled in the breakfast trolley.

Miguel could choke the cheerful young man for disturbing their magical moment. She still loved him. It shone in her eyes, and he hadn't been able to tear his gaze away from the amazing sight enough to kiss her. He'd wanted to revel in it for hours, but a magnetic force had pulled him closer.

The anticipation of finally tasting her. Savoring the full, soft texture of her lips had been within his grasp, only to be stolen by a young man doing his job.

Rather than choke the innocent fool, Miguel tipped him. The boy could forget about receiving a smile.

"You ordered too much food, Miguel," Tanya said as she lifted the tray covers.

He shrugged. "I didn't know what you liked." That wasn't true. He knew her favorite breakfast had once been waffles drenched in syrup with a side of bacon and fried eggs with the yolk barely cooked. Now that she'd lost weight, he had no idea what she'd decide to eat. The fiber-rich, tasteless cereal might be her preference for all he knew.

Air stalled in his throat as she looked up at him. "With all the dancing I did last night, I can afford a waffle or two." Then she nodded. "Once again, thanks for the water. If it hadn't been for you…"

Snatching a fresh strawberry, he held it to her lips. She hesitated for only a moment before opening her mouth, taking a bite and moaning as the juice coated her lips. Before he could break out of the spell and lick her lips clean, her tongue flicked out and did the job.

Would she run away if he kissed her? Rather than take the risk and ruin the rest of the day and night in store for them, he finished off the strawberry, understanding why the balanced, sweet yet slightly tangy flavor had brought her such pleasure.

He picked up an empty plate, handed it to her and said, "Let's eat before the food gets cold. You're going to need your energy for tonight."

Accepting the dish, her eyebrow rose. "What's on the agenda? More clubs in New York?"

A bagel, scrambled eggs, ham slices and fresh fruit made it onto his plate as he thought about how to answer. She loved surprises more than any other person he'd ever met and he didn't want to ruin this one. "Let's just say I think we've taken enough lessons away from New York to make your club awesome."

She smothered her waffles with maple syrup. "Either we're going back home, or we're moving on to a place with an even hotter nightlife. Which one is it, Astacio?"

He chuckled at her exaggerated pout. A childhood move of sliding his index finger and thumb across his lips, twisting and then tossing away the key indicated that he wouldn't reveal their plans.

"Fine. I'll wait. But can you tell me what we're doing for the rest of the afternoon? I've never been to New York before."

At the thought of providing her with yet another new experience, his excitement spilled out into a grin. "What would you like to do?"

"Go to the Empire State Building and the Statue

of Liberty." She pointed her index finger skyward. "To the tippy top of both. Oh, and Broadway and—"

He raised his hands and laughed. "Babe, we only have time for one."

She blinked up at him with a look of surprise for a moment before clearing her throat. "The Empire State Building." The enthusiasm in her tone had reduced.

"What was that look for? Is your food okay?" He spread a generous dollop of cream cheese on his bagel.

"You called me 'babe.'" She glanced at him through her lashes and giggled. Was she nervous? "I'm sure you must call everyone that since you've been doing it a lot with me lately."

He never called people by anything but their name, not even the women he'd bedded. He'd never been into the pretense of it. Never really felt it, but it had come so naturally when they'd been together. "Nope. Just you."

At her brows knitting together in confusion, he stood, leaned over the table, brushed his lips against her forehead and sank back into his seat before he could cross the barrier and kiss her the way he desired. "If you want, I could stop." Gravity would have a greater chance of failing than of him keeping his offer.

"Um…no. It's okay. I mean, it doesn't bother me." She lowered her gaze to her plate and raised a syrup-drenched waffle to her mouth.

What did it mean that she didn't mind? Damn, he hated second-guessing himself. It wasn't his style. Whatever he wanted he took, and he wanted her. Yet he kept holding back, watching her reaction to everything. Maybe she wasn't the only one who had to let go of their past. "Okay, then hurry up and finish eating." *While I fall deeper in love with you every mo-ment we're together.*

He'd keep the promise he'd made to her last night and take the art of seduction to an unforeseen level. By the time the night ended, she'd understand her position—as his woman. No more running away. For either of them.

Chapter 17

The panoramic view of the clear blue sky above New York seen from the top of the Empire State Building stole Tanya's breath. "I can't believe we're a hundred and two stories in the air." She didn't care if she looked like a tourist as she got closer to the barrier. Could she fit her head through the bars? "This is amazing. Take a picture."

He extended his arm for her camera and clicked away. "I'm glad you're enjoying it."

Today, he'd hid his true identity with the Isaac Graham costume he'd worn to observe her club on their busiest night. She smiled up at him, relaxing for the first time since they'd left the hotel. Her stomach had been tied in knots since they'd almost kissed that morning. Not enough to keep her from the scrumptious breakfast, though. Something had shifted between them and she couldn't tell if it was good or bad, so she'd kept the conversation light as they'd ridden through the streets of New York in a chauffeur-driven town car.

Stepping closer to him, she said in a low voice, "Why did Isaac make an appearance today?"

"I personify him when I want to relax and keep a really low profile."

Unable to resist, she reached up and stroked his beard-free cheek. "How come people can't recognized you? It's not like you use face masks and completely hide your features."

He turned his head and kissed the palm of her hand. The full mustache tickled, but not enough to depress the zing it sent coursing through her. He grasped her hand and interlaced her fingers with his. "I learned a long time ago that people see what they want. It's why I'm so confident that I won't be recognized no matter which disguise I wear."

They took a leisurely stroll around the periphery, mingling with the crowd gawking at the city. "I bet I'd be able to recognize you no matter what you looked like."

He squeezed her hand. "Is that so, Ms. Carrington? Should I take it as a challenge?"

She laughed as she pulled him to an empty viewing machine. "You can do whatever you want with it. But I'll always be able to tell it's you." Not just by his sexy dimples and skin that could pass for almost any cultural group because of its fine light brown tint. Miguel's aura pulsed off him. It was no wonder the cameras had loved him from such a young age. Add his outrageous lifestyle to his handsomeness and well-toned body, and he was someone no one wanted to look away from.

"Okay then. Challenge accepted. You won't know when or where, but I will thwart you."

"You can try, but it won't happen." She hesitated before releasing his large hand so she could hunt for money in her purse to see a magnified view of the city. Once the eyes of the machine popped open, she looked into it, rotating the machine at all angles to take in as much as she could.

Before long, the tower viewer clicked off. Tanya contemplated paying for another session, but she missed Miguel even though he stood only a few feet away. She turned to find him with his hand outstretched to help her down from the step. Her heart rose to her throat as she accepted his gallant offer.

"Would you like to look through another scope?" He tucked her fingers into the crook of his arm.

"I'm good. How many times have you been here?"

"This is my first time."

Tanya leaned back to look up at him. "Really?"

"I've seen the city from a helicopter a few times."

"Of course you have," she said drily. She could expect nothing less from the heir of a dynasty.

Chuckling, he stopped at an empty space that included a view of the river. "I was here on business. Not pleasure." Stepping in close behind her, he wound his arms around her waist. The warmth from his body even through his layers of clothes made her overheat in her coat as she leaned back against him.

"Have you heard from Josh?" she asked in an attempt to divert herself from fulfilling the urge to turn and press her lips against his. Why did he have such a demanding effect on her? She barely had control over herself when he was around.

Miguel stiffened. What was that about? "It's been a while, why?"

"Just wondering." She rested her head against him, hoping he'd take the invitation of her exposed neck and kiss her there. Just one would suffice. Maybe not. "Every time I see a body of water I think of him."

"I know what you mean. Bridges are his thing."

Did she have the nerve to ask? The conversation she'd had with Josh when he'd tried to get her to accept Miguel's offer had lingered in her thoughts. She'd had trouble believing it at the time, but maybe her brother hadn't been pulling her leg. "Did Josh ever..." Heat flooded her face. What was she doing?

He placed his hands on her shoulders and pivoted her to face him. His contact-lens-covered dark brown eyes looked concerned, and she felt even more embarrassed. "What?"

Now that she was staring into his too-handsome face, she couldn't ask. "Um, tell you he was dating someone? I'm worried about him. He travels so much that he might not meet anyone to settle down with. And I don't want him moving all the way across the world if he finds someone while working." *Shut up.* Clamping her lips together, she turned to look at the city, but he wouldn't let her.

His gaze pierced into her eyes. "Josh will be fine, but that's not what you were going to say."

"You still haven't told me where our next destination is."

"Woman, if you don't ask your question I'm going to—"

"What?" She quirked her lips to the side in a challenge. He'd always been able to get what he wanted from people, especially women. Yet Tanya would never relent unless she wanted to. Right now, holding her tongue and keeping things on a friendly level instead of reverting back to awkward again was a better idea than blurting out her thought.

Dipping his head closer, his breath fanned against her ear when he said, "I'll kiss you in front of all of New York." The way he nipped her earlobe had her nipples hardening.

She gulped, trying to keep her face expressionless. She had half a mind to take him up on the offer. Hell, she wanted him to follow through, but did she want their first kiss after ten years to be in public, where they'd eventually have to stop instead of make love? Would he make love to her? She'd thrown herself at him last night and he hadn't been tempted by her. Maybe his sweet words had been to lessen the blow of rejection.

Pouting, she poked a finger into his shoulder. "You are so spoiled."

His rich laughter drew attention. "I'm the youngest—and might I add, cutest—child in one of the wealthiest families in the world. Tell me you didn't expect anything different. What were you going to say?"

Unable to look him in the eyes, she focused on his chin. She may as well get it over with. "The last time I spoke to Josh, he mentioned that..." Her heart thudded hard and fast. This was crazy. Why couldn't she just spit it out? "He said he told you back in college to stay away from me."

The sigh came from deep within his chest. It must

be true. She snapped her gaze up to his, hoping he'd deny it.

"Your brother is one of a kind. He sees a person for who he is. Back then, I needed that." He rubbed his jaw. "I still need it. I live in a world with pretentious people who've always wanted something from me."

"Hey!" The protest left her mouth before she could recant it. She'd never wanted a thing from him. Other than his undying love.

Those perfect dimples appeared as he grinned down at her. "Except you. And my family, along with a very elite group of people I'd trust with my life."

Warmth radiated from chest to limbs at his admission, happy to be on such an exemplary list. *Would I have acted differently toward him if I'd known he was an Astacio from the beginning?* Without a doubt, she knew the answer was yes. But while she might've initially been starstruck, she'd have gotten over it.

He'd been the only person outside of her family and Becca who she'd been completely comfortable with. That's why she'd cried for weeks with the devastation of losing him.

The cool air rustled her hair and he smoothed the wispy strands behind her ears, lingering for a moment before releasing her. An intense magnetic draw nagged her to suck on his full bottom lip. To see if the fake mustache would scratch her skin, and to finally express the pent up passion she'd held in for so long.

"Back then, I was a mess. *Wild* doesn't even begin to describe me. I went to a strict, all-male boarding school straight through high school. When I got to college, it was as if—" he circled his open hands on either side of his head "—the freedom and being around women all the time had gone to my head. Completing my college education didn't matter. Partying, drinking and having as much sex with as many women as possible did."

Tanya cringed at the sudden pain in her chest. Why should his past hit her as if being stoned by a mob? "And then you had to deal with the rape charges."

His eyes dulled and her heart bled for him. "That was the lowest point of my life. All my friends deserted me even though I was innocent and cleared. It didn't take long for the news to follow me to Ohio State, and when Josh finally found out, he asked for my side of the story." Miguel smiled and shook his head. "That's when I knew we'd be friends for life. I couldn't do anything to jeopardize that bond."

Understanding fully dawned. "Including screwing around with his sister when he warned you not to." He'd actually broken her heart to maintain his friendship with Josh. Not because of her weight, like she'd presumed.

At least he had the decency to look sheepish by bowing his head. "Especially that. I'd lost a couple of friends in high school by messing around with their sisters. Granted, I was younger and dumber, and the only reason I even went out with them was because of easy accessibility during school breaks. The first year of college is a blur of ultimately stupid decisions and their eventual consequences. Losing Josh's friendship was out of the question."

"What about me?" Her voice trembled. The tears building behind her eyes wouldn't allow her to sound any other way. Why was ancient history bringing back the pain in full force?

She swung around, almost losing her balance as the city came into view as a blur.

What would be the point of knowing the answer to the question? They were in business together, not a romantic relationship. After his birthday bash, they'd return to being strangers. Only this time would be more devastating because of the maturity of her love for him. Yes, she'd had feelings for him before, but she'd realized over the past few days that they'd been infantile. The immensity of knowing true love weighed heavily on her chest because there would be no happily-ever-after for them.

He slipped around her. "Baby, you were the hardest thing I'd ever had to give up in my life." A soft kiss landed on her cheek just before he tucked her close to his body. "I was a stupid kid who didn't know what a wonderful woman I'd found in you. Otherwise, I would've tried to make it work between us while maintaining Josh's friendship."

She pressed her hands against his back and clung to him. He felt so right.

"I had a lot of growing up to do, and as much as I hate to admit it, I would've hurt you." He pulled away to look her in the eyes. "More than I did with my callous words."

"So you were trying to protect me by choosing Josh over me."

A flicker showed through the brown of his contact lenses. What she wouldn't give to see his true eyes at that moment. They always told the truth. "Yes. I wasn't good for you back then."

Deep in her soul, she knew they could've been happy together if he'd taken a chance on her. At least that's what her fantasies had told her. Over the years, his running around with women, partying all over the world and generally enjoying life without caring that he'd destroyed her had killed those dreams. "And now?"

He arched an artificially enhanced brow. "I'm a changed man."

"Because your parents wanted you to be."

He shook his head. "No one can make someone change. In the end, it was my decision." Stooping, he came eye to eye with her. "Don't tell the old me, but it was one of the best decisions I've ever made."

The intensity of his stare unnerved her. She let out a nervous giggle and tried to lessen the heaviness of the moment. "I wish I could go back in time. Do you remember when we had that discussion on time travel?" When uncomfortable, change the subject.

His all-seeing stare left her knees a little weak so she shifted her gaze and lifted her camera. "How about some more pictures?"

As if coming to a decision, he waited a moment before standing to his full height. "I'm a better man, Tanya. There's no other way to prove it than to be it." He reached out for the camera, and their hands touching damn near electrocuted her. "I'm ready for you."

Her heart galloped. What did he mean? Did he want her the way she'd dreamed of back in school and, to be honest, every day of her life since then? Not a day went by when he didn't cross her mind. The images varied, including one where she was shaking sense into him to the extreme opposite where she was looking up into his beautiful face while wearing an elegant lace wedding gown and pledging her love and life to him forever.

Rather than get clarification on his declaration, she angled her upper body toward the camera, pouted over her shoulder and kicked her foot behind her in a silly pose. At his laughter, the tension lightened.

"All right now, don't hurt nobody. Now give me *shocked.*" She did as he ordered. "That's it, give me *deliriously happy.*"

She smiled wide enough to show all her teeth.

The camera clicked and he looked her in the eyes. "That's it. Gorgeous. It's the look I'm expecting to see when the papers say that your club is the place to be."

He took another picture and she was sure when she spent time going through them later, she'd see love reflected in her eyes, because she felt so much of it for him. It didn't matter that they lived different lifestyles, that her brother didn't want them together, their past, or any of it.

The one thing she couldn't escape was the fact that she loved him with all her heart and would stop running scared. Maybe she'd be the one to seduce him, overwhelming tangle of fear be damned.

Chapter 18

"Welcome to Miami. Bienvenido a Miami." The Will Smith song had set itself on replay in Tanya's head from the moment the pilot said where they'd be landing.

Within the past two days, they'd flitted through the East Coast and she loved it. Almost as much as she did Miguel. No longer wishing the emotion hadn't snuck up on her, she enjoyed being with him and took advantage of his affectionate manner. They'd held hands while strolling through the bustling Manhattan streets that afternoon. She couldn't help wiping the mustard off the corner of his lip and letting her finger linger after he'd taken a bite of a piping hot pretzel.

And she'd already become spoiled by his complete attention. There had only been a few times when he'd taken a call regarding work, and he'd kept the conversations short. When they'd reached the hotel room to get their things, she'd found three more outfits lying on her bed.

The glimmering gold dress with adorable capped sleeves had called out to her even though it was more revealing in the chest area than she was accustomed to and only reached to the top of her knees. The dress had glided over her curves as if it had been designed solely for her.

The other two pieces were day dresses. Since she'd worn her travel-home outfit to roam New York, she appreciated Miguel's thoughtfulness at providing her with more. The man certainly knew how to take care of a woman. *He's had enough practice.* That snide voice couldn't have been hers.

Sure he'd been seen with more women than she found comfortable, but he'd changed. He'd said he had. The media thought so, too. But what if he'd been going out with the women under different guises like he'd done with her? What if he was still trying to date every female in the world? Her included? And then once he had her, he'd dump her?

She'd quivered in fear at the thought. Yes, she'd fallen for him, but he wasn't hers. No matter what happened, she'd have to remember that. At least they had these next few weeks together while getting her club set up. It would have to be enough.

They stepped out the limo in front of the brightest building Tanya had ever seen. The white paint reflected the bright multicolored lights waving around. "This is different from New York."

Miguel placed a hand against her lower back, sending a tremor through her. She felt both protected and sexy. Maybe she should've taken that first slinky low-backed jumpsuit she'd refused to try on. At least then he'd be setting her skin ablaze with direct contact and not just through the thin material.

Miguel had surprised her with another costume. She detested the thick sideburns, and the dreaded contact lenses were in place, making his eyes a cool chocolate brown. At least he'd used a thinner mustache this time. His curls were covered with a stylish white brimmed hat that matched his bright red suit, and a shimmery white silk shirt exposed chest hair she longed to glide her fingers through. A thick gold chain completed his look.

"Are you sure they'll let a pimp in here?" Tanya asked.

He laughed. "Look around, I fit right in."

A scan of the people waiting in the long line to get into the club told her he was correct. At least for the guys who seemed to have left their college days behind years ago.

Miguel, Carlos Diaz for the night, went straight to the door, spoke in fluent Spanish to the bouncer and without question they were let in. She had no idea which shocked her more, the chameleon she was hanging out with or the bright colorful lights in the club that assaulted her. The exterior should've been enough warning.

She assessed the first floor, expecting something different from the clubs they'd been to in New York. The enthusiastic dancers gyrated to a reggaeton song blasting as she and Miguel made their way up the stairs. Nothing stood out that she'd want to implement

in her club. She reminded herself of the great name
she'd come up with and had yet to share with Miguel.

In the VIP section, she settled into the couch. When
Miguel sat so close their knees touched, she forgot
what she'd wanted to tell him as the heat from his
body seeped into her.

"What can I get you to drink?" the server asked.
For the first time, it was a male, and yet he still ogled
Miguel as if he wanted to take him home.

No such luck, buddy. Why did it bother her so much
that everyone wanted her man? *He's nowhere near to
being my man.* It didn't stop the jealousy from making her scoot closer and placing a hand on his knee.

She glanced up at Miguel for a moment and had
trouble swallowing when even through the contact
lenses desire flared from his eyes and landed in her
lower belly.

"A drink?" the server repeated.

"Two sparkling waters," Miguel said while still
holding her captive with his gaze. "Unless you want
something stronger."

What she wanted was to get out of the noisy club
and continue the relaxing day they'd shared. Her mind
wrestled with the idea of seducing him. She'd never
done it before and was scared of his rejection, but her
body longed for him to make love to her. The way
he'd touched her all day told her he'd be receptive,
but she'd thought the same thing back in college just
before she'd gotten shot down.

Tanya shook her head, releasing herself from his
hypnotic effect. "It'll be a while before I drink alcohol again. Water is fine."

They didn't speak while absorbing the ambiance

of the VIP area. The owners had spared no expense in furnishing the place. The leather seats reeked of money. That's not the way Miguel wanted to go with their club. She sucked in a sharp breath. When had she started considering him as a true co-owner?

"So what do you think?" he asked.

"It's nice." She leaned in closer, taking in the citrus-and-sandalwood scent emanating from him. "To be honest, they all seem the same. Large space, good lighting and a DJ that can get everyone on the dance floor." Her jaw dropped open. "Is that Emilio Stewart?"

Miguel flicked his gaze in the direction she was drooling toward. The megastar sat surrounded by a gaggle of women fawning over him. "Sure is. I'd go over and say hi, but he doesn't know me as Carlos. We used to hang out back in the day."

She ordered her mouth to close. "Each of the clubs had stars or musicians popping in, and you claimed to know them all."

He shrugged. "It was part of the party brand I created for myself back then. I'm rich and popular, and it was just as good for them to be seen with me as it was for me to be seen with them. Win-win."

"And that's why your birthday party will make Destiny skyrocket."

"Destiny?"

She nodded enthusiastically. "The name of our club." There was that joint pronoun again.

"Try again, sweetheart. 'Destiny' isn't it."

The server came over, set down their drinks and took off. Tanya presumed the scowl she directed at him wasn't inviting for more flirtation. "Why not?"

He took a drink of the water. "I'm just not feeling it."

One day, she'd be able to shoot laser beams from her eyes, but for the moment, a narrow-eyed glare would have to suffice. "What if I am?"

"I'm taking veto power."

She sighed, knowing the name wouldn't adorn the front of her club. "Which you've done for each one I've presented."

He stood and reached a hand down to her. "Come up with an acceptable one and I won't reject it. Let's dance."

Answering the call of the beat, yet still annoyed with him for his arrogant behavior, she ignored his offer. Standing on her own, she sauntered ahead of him to the dance floor. Her irritation faded when he stepped up behind her, placed his hands on her hips and leaned into her.

Her body responded by moving to his initiated rhythm, loving that even though the music was loud enough to blast an eardrum she still heard the groan he emitted.

After their first club of the night, Miguel couldn't grind up on Tanya again. He'd never known such frustrated desire for any woman. With her luscious, curvaceous body, she'd set him on fire. He'd cut the club tour short, ending after the third because if he didn't get her into his bed soon, he'd explode.

Who knew that wanting to make a woman completely his would jack up his desire for her? He craved her touch. Three years ago, he would've been freaked-out, but now he was ready to have her in his life full-time. Would she accept him after what he'd put her through? He'd told her how much he'd changed, but did she believe him?

For Tanya, he was more than willing to prove himself.

"How about 'Thrive'?" She threw it at him as they stepped into her room.

Laughing, he pulled off his hat and pushed his fingers through his hair, releasing the curls. "Isn't that the name of the second club we just came from?"

"Exactly. It works for them so it will for us, too."

He stepped into her space. Even after all the dancing they'd done, her honeysuckle fragrance still lingered enough to entice. "That's not how it works."

She moved backward and propped a hand on her hip. "What do you suggest we call the place, Mr. Rebrander, since my ideas aren't good enough?"

Her skittishness didn't make seducing her easy, but it made him happy. She had to be feeling the heated attraction drawing him to her. After the way he'd reacted to her dancing against him for the past two days, she had to know he wanted her. "I didn't say the names weren't good—they just don't strike me as right."

After raising her hands into the air, she let them drop to her sides with a light smack against her thighs. "I can't read your eyes with those horrible contact lenses in. Please take them out."

"Come with me." He offered his hand. She didn't reach for him. "The condoms are in my room." He'd taken a risk with his directness.

Her face scrunched into an expression of pain for the briefest moment before she snorted and crossed her arms over her chest instead of running into his arms like he'd expected. "If you're going to have sex with one of the women who tried desperately to catch your attention at the club then you'll need to go get them."

Dropping his hand, he looked her straight in the eyes. "You're the only one I want to be with." *Tonight, tomorrow, forever.* He hoped she could hear his heart screaming out to her. They'd be good together. But how could he articulate it without her thinking he was crazy? They'd only gotten reacquainted over a few short weeks. Was it enough time to know she was the one person he wanted to spend the rest of his life with? *Yes.*

He could see her mind vacillating on the decision. Just when he swore she was about to agree, her eyes narrowed. "Are you playing a joke on me, Astacio?"

With no other way to prove how much he wanted her, he got into her face and touched his lips to hers. No sweetness existed as he delved his tongue into her mouth and she gasped in surprise. No teasing as he'd expected their second-chance kiss to possess. Passion drove him to glide his tongue against hers. His heart swelled when she grabbed his shoulders and dragged him even closer as she responded.

He groaned as he angled her head to drink in more of her. Her hands found their way into his hair and rubbed his scalp. Heat flared in his groin. With the strength of a thousand men, he broke off the kiss and panted while he once again held out his hand. "It's you I want. Come with me."

This time, without hesitation, she clasped his hand and he could've floated out of the room with her. Not wasting any time, he swooped her up and marched to the door.

Wrapping her arms around his neck, she held on tight. "Put me down. I'm too heavy."

"Not for me. Remember back in college when I gave you that piggyback ride? I'll always be able to carry you."

She relaxed her grip and rested her head on his shoulder. She felt so right with her body against him.

He reached down, opened the door, and they left her room. "Reach into my inner breast pocket for my keycard and open my door," he said seconds later when they reached his place.

Inside the threshold, he set her down and peppered kisses along her neck, stopping at the bounding pulse to suck the sensitive flesh. Her whimpers of pleasure drove him to grasp the hem of her dress and pull it upward as he savored the exquisite salty taste of her skin.

And then it came to a crashing halt as she pushed his hands away when he'd touched her hips.

Dazed with desire, he asked, "What's wrong?"

Her husky voice turned him on even more. "I like my body."

"I do, too." He smiled and reached for her, but she eluded him with a step backward.

Holding her hand to her belly, she rubbed the area. "I worked hard to lose all that weight and I'm proud of my accomplishment, but I'm not perfect. If you're expecting to see hip bones and abdominal muscles, you'll be disappointed. And..." She swallowed hard and looked down at her shoes.

Not letting her get away again, he framed her face

with his hands and tilted her head up at him. "What is it, baby?"

She sucked in a shaky breath. "Broderick was the last man I slept with, and that was a year before he asked for a divorce." Her gaze held his as if she needed him to know the absolute truth. Miguel steeled himself for whatever she had to share.

"He was an attentive husband, maybe overly so at times, and had tried to anticipate my needs. He made our marriage almost perfect, but, our intimate life was boring and infrequent. At first, I thought it was my body, so that took a toll on me psychologically."

His teeth hurt from clenching his jaw. The selfish bastard should've been honest with her from the moment he'd found out he was gay instead of stringing her along. He knelt before her and kissed her belly through her clothes as he gripped her hips.

His hands roamed to her perky breasts and palmed them. Getting to his feet, he found her nipples through her dress and pinched them. Her sharp inhale made him harder. He grabbed her ass and slammed her into him. "Do you feel what you do to me?" He ground himself into her lower abdomen. "I find you irresistible. Beautiful. When I'm with you, I think about making love to you. When we're apart, my mind is occupied with being around you. I..." He stopped himself from professing his love. He doubted she'd believe him. "Crave you. Desire you. Need you. Ever since college. No matter what's under your clothes, I'll still want you. I promise."

Looking into his eyes, she nodded, and at that moment he became the happiest man in the world.

Chapter 19

"I hate that you have to hide your eyes," Tanya said, trying to put on a casual air while watching Miguel remove his contact lenses at her insistence. Her stomach did a cycle of clenching and looping. Were they really about to have sex? How could they not after the impassioned declaration he'd just made.

He turned toward her. Had he really removed the contact lenses? His eyes were still dark, dilated with desire as he came toward her. Her heart hammered. This time there was no trying to justify or back out. She was in love with the man and no matter what happened, she'd accept it for the rest of her life.

Closing the space between them, he placed his hands on her waist and squeezed. "I explained the necessity of the disguises." His brows creased together in concern. "Don't you believe me?"

This uncertain man wasn't the same arrogant one she'd known years ago. He had never doubted himself or that anyone else would, either. And yet his humility made him even sexier. With a newfound boldness, she looped her arms around his neck. "I do, but it doesn't mean I have to like it."

As a response, he kissed her. She couldn't get enough of the full soft texture of his lips and melted as he dipped his tongue into her mouth. She responded like a woman who'd been starved from her favorite food for years, tasting, savoring and laving him up as if it would be her last opportunity.

In the back of her mind she became aware of them moving, but didn't realize they were next to the shower until the sound of water penetrated.

"I don't want to be apart from you for a minute," he moaned as he tugged at her lower lip. "So we're going to take a shower together."

Stiffening, she tried to back out of his arms with a fierce head shake. She'd never showered with anyone before—that was just too much physical disclosure.

Miguel wouldn't allow her to slither away. "I see I'll have to convince you about how beautiful you are."

"Oh, I know I'm beautiful." He wasn't the only one who could be cocky. "I've never had a problem with my face. My body, on the other hand…" She pivoted toward the bedroom in an attempt to escape.

He tugged her close and when his lips landed on her neck and lapped at her skin, her knees lost all structure and she clung to him.

"Mmm. Salty and delicious." He nipped at her shoulder. "So you'd like me to lick you clean? I can work with that."

Her eyes flung open at his proposal and she huffed out a breath. The damn man knew how to get his way in all things. "Fine."

That's all he needed to reach down to the hem of her dress and slide it up her body, exposing her thick thighs, purple lace-and-satin panties hugging her wide hips, stomach, nipped waist and lace-covered full breasts. Miguel sucked in a breath as she chewed on her bottom lip.

"We might just skip the shower. You're amazing."

His words settled something within her heart, bringing her a sense of relief. Her panties became even wetter with her desire. Pleased, she smiled wide as she pointed to the running water. "Maybe we should hop in before an environmental protection representative comes after us." Never in her wildest dreams would she have guessed she'd be comfortable enough to crack a joke while in a near-naked state.

She was so caught up in staring at Miguel as he stripped that she forgot to take the rest of her own clothes off. He'd filled out since she'd seen him shirtless back in college. She reached out and ran her hand along his chest and down his bicep, eliciting a hissed inhale. When he pulled down his trousers and boxer briefs, her mouth went dry as she witnessed what had poked her as they'd danced.

Hypnotized with an incredible need, she reached for him. Instead of allowing her to touch, he grasped her wrists and kissed each of her palms. "Let's get you naked."

He unclasped her bra and slid it down her arms, freeing her breasts into his awaiting hands. Before she understood his intention, he bent and pulled one of the hardened peaks into his mouth. She whispered his name as she dug her nails into his shoulders, fearing she'd fall with the ecstasy. He switched to the other and her body went insane, arching her back and holding his head in place. She never wanted the pleasure to end.

Then it did. He pulled her into the water and joined her. They were silent as they explored each other's bodies with their lathered hands. She gloried in every perfect muscle he possessed as he smoothed his hands up and down her body as if worshipping her.

When he reached the apex of her thighs, she groaned when he slid his fingers along the outside of her, then pushed his thumb between her folds and stroked. She jumped and landed with her back against the stall's wall at the intimacy of his touch.

He continued rubbing, making her whimper. She didn't even care that her hair was getting wet. His ministrations felt so good. Then he slid a finger inside and the sensations jacked up ten levels. All she could do was hold on to him so she wouldn't send them tumbling.

When his mouth found her nipple again, he sucked hard, and she exploded in a way she'd never experienced before. The orgasm lasted forever, and when she came back to reality, he had her wrapped in his arms.

"You were stunning," he whispered. "I will see you come again. Next time, I'll be buried deep inside you."

Unable to understand how she'd be able to experience such a thing again without slipping into a coma, she leaned heavily against him as he turned off the water. After grabbing a towel, he took his time dry-ing her in the steamy room, and then did a rush job on himself while she drank in every inch of his incredible body.

The thousands of fantasies he'd had over the years couldn't have prepared Miguel for actually being with Tanya. Bringing her to climax had been one of the most pleasurable experiences of his life, and his body had become impossibly harder.

Once he'd laid her on the bed after their shared shower, she'd fallen asleep. Content to have her anywhere near him, he'd watched her for the past half an hour in utter amazement. He kissed his sleeping woman's shoulder. *Mine.* His brain roared as if he needed reminding. He'd known it since forever, but immaturity and insecurities on both sides had kept them apart. Not anymore.

"Baby," he whispered into her ear just before nipping it. She raised her hands above her head, exposing her delectable breasts to his hungry eyes. Her arched stretch brought the succulent dark brown nipples closer to him. An offering. He ignored the summons and returned his gaze to her face. "Tanya."

Her eyes popped open to meet his and then widened before glancing down at her naked body covered to hip level with a sheet. She reached down to pull up the cloth, but he stilled her hand by interlacing her fingers with his. "Don't hide from me, sweetheart."

She ducked her head and then snapped it up again. "Oh, my goodness. I fell asleep and you're still…"

He wiggled his eyebrows and winked. "Bet you didn't know I could put it on you so good."

Giggling, she shifted onto her side to face him. "That's what you get for not letting me touch you."

He rubbed their noses together before dipping his head to taste her. He indulged in the sweet texture of her tongue against his as she wrapped her arm around him and brought him closer. He pulled back so their lips brushed. "I didn't mind. Your pleasure was more important."

He could feel rather than see the smile on her lips when she kissed him. He groaned when her hand slid between them and stroked the part of him that needed her most. The touch was initially tentative and then she started exploring. It had been too long since he'd had sex. If she continued, he'd come in her hand instead of inside her body where he longed to be.

Pulling himself away from her tantalizing lips and touch, he went to his suitcase and pulled out a box of condoms from the side pocket. Maybe he enjoyed the way her gaze devoured him from head to toe a little too much. He rushed back to her side and jumped onto the bed. Was he being too enthusiastic? He didn't care. He'd waited years for this moment. To be with the woman he loved. Had always loved.

He pulled out a packet from the box, opened it and slipped the condom on. She'd been so fascinated with the process that she'd left her body bare for him to feast on. He prepared to enjoy holding on to her curves as he drove into her over and over again. Anticipating the feel of her strong thighs wrapping around him as they joined in the most intimate way two people could.

He loomed over her until she lay flat on her back. Bracing his hands on the outside of her breasts, he pushed them together and wished he could indulge by placing both nipples in his mouth at the same time. Instead, he grazed his lips along the underside of her breast until he reached his destination. Rounding his tongue against one nipple, he smiled as she grabbed the back of his head and pushed him toward his intended goal.

Writhing beneath him as he suckled one breast while rolling the other nipple between his fingers, she emitted whimpers of need that drove him. He gave the other mound the same attention with his mouth. By the time his hand slid down her belly to her tempting center, the smell of her arousal had his nostrils flaring.

He looked down at her as he slid a finger into her before circling her bud. "Do you know how wet you are?"

His vixen gave him his answer by opening her legs wider as she ground against his finger with a loud moan. "Please, Miguel."

"What do you want me to do to you?"

Their gazes locked. "Come inside me. I need you."

The words had him between her legs in a flash. He kissed her as he slid slowly into her. Nothing else had ever felt so right. So complete. He pulled out to the tip before filling her again. He couldn't maintain the slow pace for long, not when she met him with each stroke.

Speeding up their rhythm, he stared at her. "Open your eyes."

When they fluttered open, she smiled and his heart leaped. Increasing their rhythm, he plunged into her.

The initial tightening of her inner walls urged him to delve into her faster and harder. When she cried out his name, her clenching shelter pulled an orgasm from him so intense he ended up lying on her with his full weight.

She didn't seem to mind, because she held on to him.

When he found the strength to lift himself up, he gazed into her glowing face. No one should be so beautiful. Still joined, he spoke the words he'd never said to any other woman. Now he knew they'd always been reserved for her. "I love you."

Chapter 20

A smile and a brief kiss on the lips after Miguel's declaration was all she could give him before claiming she had to use the bathroom. She'd panicked, wanting to tell him how deeply she cared, but couldn't. Had it just been the sex talking? Something he said to all his conquests? Her heart had soared for a brief moment as she hung on to every word, and then her brain had brought logic into the equation and deflated the moment.

She was annoyed with herself for allowing her self-doubts and the differences in their social statuses to keep her from basking in his professed love. Her attention caught on the shower stall. Would she ever be able to feel water slide against her skin without thinking about his passion-inducing touch?

Hell, she had difficulty not thinking about him

with every breath. She didn't hold out hope she'd get over him any time soon when he decided to leave her for someone classier, richer, slimmer and more glamorous.

"What time are we leaving?" she asked when she stepped out of the bathroom wearing the hotel's fluffy white robe. She prayed she hadn't made things uncomfortable between them. The ego was a fragile, living thing, and she hoped she hadn't injured his to the point of destroying their newfound friendship.

To her surprise, he strode over to her, bare-chested, last night's trousers slung low on his lean hips, and mushed her against him. "I meant what I said, Tanya. I love you. I've always loved you, and nothing can or will ever change that. You can't run from what we have forever, but I'll give you time."

Her heart screamed the words of adoration back at him, but they got stuck in her clogged throat. What if he hadn't changed? Could people change? She had her doubts.

Rather than admit to her feelings, she pulled back and changed the subject. "I have the perfect name for the club."

His eyes filled with what she swore was disappointment. And then he gave her his teasing grin, showing off her two most favorite dimples in the world. "Let me guess." He tapped a finger to his lips. "'Club Dance-A-Lot'? No, wait. 'Club Drink-It-Up'?"

She laughed at his silliness. His lovemaking had been the catalyst. The name had popped into her head when she'd drifted back down to find herself in the arms of the man she loved so much that she felt his presence in every cell of her body. "How about… 'Fervor'?"

His eyes brightened as the corners of his mouth tilted up even more. He kissed her hard on the lips, lifted her and swung her around. "It's perfect."

"Put me down, Miguel." She struggled to get the words out through her giggles.

He settled her on her feet and splayed his hands along her hips. "How did you come up with it?"

I love you with a white-hot fervor that I have to deny. At least for now. She attempted to smooth her wild mess of hair. "It just came to me."

He beamed. "It's brilliant. I can already see it hanging on the building with its white glow and red outline."

His enthusiasm was contagious, and she could envision it along with the ideas he'd mentioned last week. This trip had opened her eyes to what her club lacked and she was grateful for the revelation. Unable to help herself, she grasped his face between her hands and kissed him. "Thank you so much. I can finally see your vision and it's going to be wonderful. Broderick will be so jealous."

Miguel's jaw clenched and his eyes darkened like they always did when she brought up her ex. "This is about making what you own a success, not about him. By the way, we have a lot to discuss on the jet. We're taking off in about an hour so we'd better get going."

Their oasis of bliss had ended. The real world would interfere with whatever they'd created and shared. The love he'd expressed would be lost to her forever. Even if he hadn't really meant it, the temporary knowledge that he'd proclaimed his love sent warmth spreading through her chest. Should she take the risk and tell him how she felt or stay safe by holding it in?

Would she ever be ready to take the leap? What could she truly offer him? And what would the tabloids say when they found out he was seeing a nobody like her? She'd be crucified, and his reputation might suffer because of it.

Stepping out of his reach, she nodded. "I'll be ready in ten minutes. Thank you for the clothes and the trip of a lifetime."

He held his arms out wide. "This is just the beginning." With those words he turned and left the room.

If only it were true. He'd probably find her interesting for the short time they had to refurbish the club, but after that, he'd lose interest, just like he had with all the others. At least this time she'd be ready to be tossed away.

Relaxing into the jet's bucket seat, Miguel looked out the window as the plane approached Cleveland. The conversation had consisted of the changes they'd make to the club. He liked that they were on the same page and ready to move things forward.

What he didn't care for was her reluctance to fire her club manager. Although the financial report his sister had emailed to him that afternoon didn't show he'd been tampering with the money, Miguel still didn't trust him. He couldn't understand why Tanya refused to even consider letting him go when the man was so useless at his job. Did she have feelings for Clint? The rage of jealousy that had filled him was superseded by a sense of calm. The woman he knew wouldn't have given herself to him if she were in love with another man. Would she?

"Why won't you fire the club manager?" Miguel had asked.

Crossing her arms over her chest, her lips had thinned and she'd remained silent.

His ire had risen. "I'm warning you—if you don't get rid of him now, he'll destroy your business." Maybe he should've chosen his words better because all she did was squint her eyes at him and maintain her silence.

Drawing in a deep breath, he held it for a count of five. How had he forgotten just how stubborn the woman could be? The quality he appreciated least about her. Rather than make things worse, he'd left it alone until now, because the issue had to be dealt with. "I can fire him if that's what's bothering you."

A weaker man would've shrunk back at her narrow-eyed glower and snarl. He didn't flinch. At least not so she could see. He stared right back.

"Not only is he a friend," she said, "but he's the only one who stuck by me when Broderick left." Her shoulders slumped. "Two weeks after the divorce, I was feeling so lonely and depressed that I went to the club just to get out of the house. I ended up in the office bawling. Clint came in and, instead of leaving me at my most hysterical, he sat without saying a word. His presence strengthened me. When the tears had abated he told me I was one of the strongest people he'd ever met and that I deserved more than Broderick. Those words buoyed me and cemented our friendship."

Her gaze softened. "He always asked if I needed

to talk. On the few occasions that I took him up on the offer, he really listened. I've only known him as a good man." She hung her head, stealing away their eye contact. "I'm having a tough time believing he stayed with me only to mess up my life."

Being deceived by a friend was a thousand times worse than with a stranger. Miguel still didn't like the guy, but he'd gained a level of respect for the compassion he'd shown to Tanya. It didn't change anything where the club was concerned. "Sometimes you have to let people go."

"It doesn't make it any easier." She looked straight into his eyes. "Especially when you find it almost impossible to trust in the first place."

Was she talking about what he'd done to her years ago? What he'd apologized for? The one thing he regretted more than anything else he'd ever done? Ignoring the Fasten Seat Belt sign that had come on a few minutes ago, Miguel undid his seat belt, knelt before her and squeezed her hands.

"I don't know what to say. I did this, and I will apologize for the rest of my life if that's what you need to move on. All I know is that I'm a different man than I was then and I'm ready to prove it to you. To commit to you."

He ignored her gasp. "I love you, Tanya. It wasn't the heat of the moment speaking back in the hotel room. I've loved you since the first time we argued back in college. I'm sorry I took away your ability to trust others."

She blinked at him a few times, opened and closed her mouth, and then slammed back against the seat and smiled. Not one of joy and celebration but one that he suspected to be a combination of amusement and disbelief. "You are one arrogant man. I've already forgiven you. You do remember the guy who married me and left me for another man right? He played pretend for almost three years and I believed it." She shook her head and planted a kiss on his cheek.

Stunned, speechless and more than a little confused, he got up and sat in his seat.

She shook her head. "Not everything is about you, Miguel."

He relaxed with his relief. At least she didn't blame him. Maybe he did take their past a little too seriously. He should've known she'd forgiven him when she said she had.

With a hand to her chest, she grinned. "Thanks for the sweet words, too."

He sobered. Had she just thanked him for professing his love? Now that hurt. If the past wasn't their issue, why hadn't she told him she loved him? It was written in her eyes and on her face when she looked at him. Perhaps he was seeing what he wanted and she didn't love him. He rubbed the area over his heart, trying to relieve the tightness that had come from nowhere.

"Are you in love with your club manager?" He just had to know.

The humor left her eyes and trepidation filled him at the potential of her answer. He'd never been so afraid of a response in his life. He didn't do fear often, but it overwhelmed him now.

"You're an interesting man, Mr. Astacio." She shook her head. "Do you really think I could make love to one man while being in love with another?"

All he heard in her sentence was that she loved him. Okay, maybe he'd jumped a few steps ahead, but at least she wasn't in love with her smarmy club manager. Even if she didn't have feelings for him yet, Miguel would do everything in his power to make sure she would.

His heart lighter and renewed with hope, he stated, "So that's a no then. Will you fire him or should I?"

His eyes were drawn to her incredible breasts as they rose and fell with the exasperation flowing from her. He held up both hands, knowing that, in his attempt to win her over, pissing her off wouldn't help. "Fine, handle it your way."

At her heartwarming smile, he realized he was a goner. He'd do anything to make her happy. Absolutely anything.

Chapter 21

"I called Broderick yesterday," Tanya admitted to Becca as they waited for their breakfast order to arrive.

"Get out!" If the woman had been standing next to her rather than sitting across the table, Tanya may have been shoved off her feet. "Why?"

Tanya flopped back into her seat. A week after their return from Florida and she'd gotten up the nerve to find out more about Clint from her ex-husband. "Not to ask how he's doing, that's for sure." She angled her head. "Although we did have a pleasant conversation once my reason for calling was out of the way."

Becca rolled her eyes. "Which was?"

"To get information about Clint. Deep down, I know Miguel is right and I should fire him, but I need a legitimate reason. After all, I do consider him a friend."

"So did you get one?"

Boy, did she. "You won't believe why Broderick promoted Clint to manager." Knowing how much her friend loved drama, she paused to take a sip of juice. "The weasel found Broderick and his business partner—now husband—in a compromising position a few months before he presented the divorce papers. Clint threatened to tell me if he wasn't promoted to manager. Broderick basically managed the place anyway, so it didn't disturb his flow of money."

Becca picked up her dropped jaw from the table. "Oh, my goodness. Who knew Clint could be so damn sneaky?"

Tanya sighed. "Once again, I was duped by someone I trusted."

"Technically, he was playing Broderick. At least he wasn't stealing from you. Only running your business into the ground. That's a plus."

She waved her hands in the air and said, "Yippee," in the driest tone she could muster.

"Why didn't Broderick tell you once he filed for divorce?"

"Because my fantastic ex-husband didn't know how to keep it in his pants when around his true love, so Clint got pictures and threatened to expose him to the world. It would've still affected me." She slapped her hands over her face. "Can you imagine how embarrassing that would've been?"

"At least now you know, right?" Becca encouraged. "There's no reason not to fire his behind. I'd opt for hiring someone to kick it first, though."

Tanya laughed. "Miguel's instincts were right on point. I just wish I'd listened sooner. I think Clint knows something's going down because he took a few days off from work."

"Girl, you know where he lives. Hunt him down and fire him so you don't have to deal with his conniving ways a minute longer. I'm sure big bad Miguel would be more than happy to assist you."

Why hadn't she taken Miguel up on his offer to do the dirty work for her? It would've made things so much easier. Her pride had forced her to stick to her guns. It wasn't his club, although she'd started thinking about it as a partnership.

Becca waited while the waitress set their food on the table. "You and Miguel did the deed, and you're head over heels in love with him. Which I warned you to avoid, but you *never* listen to me."

Tanya sat speechless. "How the f—" She caught herself just in time from being a horrible example to a five-year-old sitting at the next table. "How did you know?"

"There's nobody in this world—" Becca waved a fork in her direction "—not even your fine brother who knows you as well as me. I haven't seen you look this happy in years. Senior year of college to be exact when Mr. Cool hopped into your life."

"He told me he loved me."

"What?" Becca coughed and reached for her water.

Although it had been amazing, she wouldn't count the declaration he'd said right after they'd made love. The one she'd cherish most was the one in the plane even though she'd laughed. Sex had been taken out of the equation, he'd been more than a little pissed at her stubbornness, and yet he'd let her know how much she meant to him. She'd never felt so treasured in her life. "A few times actually."

Becca's dark eyes went wide. "And…"

She tipped a spoonful of sugar into her oatmeal. "I couldn't bring myself to say it back."

"Even though you do."

"Exactly."

"That's what he gets for messing around the first time." Becca shook her head. "How can he expect you to lay your heart bare after squishing it to oblivion?"

"It's not like that. I've forgiven him for what he did to me in the past." She ate her oats, letting the comforting warmth distract her.

"So what stopped you?"

Shrugging, Tanya pushed away the food. "We're worlds apart."

"Um, correct me if I'm wrong here, but he hasn't grown any poorer since college and neither have you. In fact, you're closer economically than you were back then." Her friend frowned. "Granted, he's mega-rich, and you're, well…not. But what's changed? This didn't bother you in college."

"I was young with a crush. Now, I get the impression things could get serious." Or had already passed that point, rushing her along with the current. She sighed out her frustration.

Her friend arched a brow. "So you want to maintain a light, sex-only relationship?"

Would it be a bad thing? The sex was phenomenal. The best of her life. They'd made love every night this week. Maintaining the whole friends-with-benefits deal would make life simpler, at least for the time being, but she had a feeling Miguel wouldn't go for it. He was an all-in kind of man. He'd made it known he wanted her, and by any means necessary he'd have her. "How will his family react? The world?"

"I know you aren't saying you'd give him up because of what people will think. What happened to the fearless woman I look up to? You shouldn't give a rat's tail about anything or anyone. Concentrate on what you feel. What does your gut say?"

Before Tanya could speak, Becca held up a hand. "It's not for me to hear. It's for you to ponder. If you want to be with him, then go for it. The opinions of the world be damned. You only have one life. Live it. Don't let anyone stop you from getting yours."

She didn't even need to think about it. As always, Becca was right. She wanted Miguel. She always had and always would. Wasn't that why she'd married another man? Because she'd known subconsciously she'd never be able to love him like she had Miguel, and he wouldn't feel badly about never having her true affection?

Okay, maybe she was going over the line and taking the culpability away from Broderick, who'd leaped way beyond deceptive. At least she hadn't done it intentionally.

Picking up her spoon with renewed interest in her daily fiber source, she ate. With her body feeling lighter as the full truth of Becca's words sank in, nothing could keep her from what she desired, not even herself. If she and Miguel were meant to be together, then she wouldn't stand in her own way to happiness.

The one thing Miguel had tried to prevent by wearing those disguises stared up at him. Not even on the computer, but in black-and-white print. He slammed the base of a fist onto his desk. Not just one tabloid, but every single one his assistant could get his hands on had printed the story as front-page news.

He'd had Tanya's number on constant redial with no answer. Hanging up one last time, he cursed. Where could she be so early in the morning? He'd kept her up late last night making love before she'd kicked him out of her bed and into his car. He still couldn't understand why she refused to let him spend the night.

They'd established a routine since returning from their club-hopping excursion. He'd go to work and daydream about her all day, head to the club in his full mustache costume as Isaac Graham, work on the club to make sure things were going smoothly for their opening and then they'd head to her place. He couldn't get enough of her. If he could quit his job and spend every moment with her, he would.

He might have to once his father saw the debacle he'd gotten embroiled in. He'd been so close to becoming the new Executive Public Relations Officer. Now he could kiss the job goodbye. Raking his hands through his hair, he reminded himself to deal with one problem at a time. He had to find Tanya and get her to a safe, paparazzi-free zone. Did any such place exist these days?

He'd already dispatched members of the Astacios' security team to both her home and the club. They had reported she wasn't at either location. Where could she be? Pacing proved useless in finding her, but his restless legs wouldn't allow him to sit for more than a few minutes at a time. He blamed himself. He must've slipped up somehow. After six months of hiding behind some damn good disguises and only popping up to the press when it suited him, how had they found out?

On the verge of running out of his office to search for his woman, he answered Tanya's special ringtone on the first ring. "Are you okay? Where are you?"

"I'm fine, but what the hell is going on? There are people with cameras all over the club. I had to sneak in the back way."

Tension left his shoulders at the sound of her calm voice. Was this what it was to care about someone? To not be able to relax until he knew she was safe? "Good. Stay right where you are and don't open the door. Is anyone with you?"

"My restaurant staff. They didn't open for breakfast because they had no idea what was going on. What is this, Miguel?"

Would she leave him once she read all the terrible things they'd written about her? He swiped a hand down his face as anxiety made an uncomfortable reappearance. The truth. She'd always appreciated it. "Someone found out about my disguises."

Her gasp traveled through the phone, but he continued on with the worst part of the news. "They also figured out who you are and spread malicious information about you to the tabloids."

He heard the scraping of a chair against the floor. "Oh, my God. How? Who?"

"I don't know, but I'm going to find out and make the bastard pay. But first, I need to make sure you're okay, and I can only do that if you're with me." He did what came naturally and took charge by texting a quick message to Roland on his other phone to pick her up, resisting the urge to rush to her side. It would only make things worse. "I'm sending my bodyguard over to get you. Will you close the restaurant?"

"No. It's my only moneymaker right now." She let out what sounded like a nervous giggle. "Although now that it's out that we're associated, the club will take off, even if people are just curious to see me."

Was she freaking out? He'd never seen her under pressure. No real stress, other than what he'd put her through back in college, and he'd had to turn away from her pain then. "Babe, Roland, my guard, will be at your back door in a minute. Don't have your staff open the place until he gets you out of there."

"Okay."

"I want you to promise me something." The last thing either of them needed was for her to check the internet and read the viciousness they'd written.

"What?"

His request was likely to make her do the opposite of what he asked, but he had to warn her. "Please stay away from the internet and don't answer the phone unless it's from me."

"Fine."

Stunned, he sank into his seat. "No argument?"

She laughed. "I'm not always difficult. This is your world and I'm kind of flipping out. I've never had people chasing me to take pictures or ask questions. It's not a fun experience. Much more stressful than watching celebrities go through it."

"I'll fix this." He held a hand to his chest. "I promise." And he meant it. He'd always sought the spotlight, but she'd lived a quiet, private life. The fact that she wasn't screaming at him showed how much class and strength she possessed, and his respect for her rose even higher. He looked down at the message that came through on his other phone. "Roland says he's there. You can trust him. He'll bring you right to me."

"Okay. Thanks, Miguel."

For what? He was the one who had gotten her into this chaos. He'd hoped to ease her into his life, not thrust her into the spotlight on center stage.

Miguel stopped at his assistant's desk on the way out of his office. "Cancel all my meetings. Not that they'll be able to get up here, but you have my permission to Taser anyone who even seems like paparazzi."

Franklin laughed.

He'd instructed Roland to take Tanya to the most secure place Miguel knew. His home. He ducked into the elevator to the garage-floor parking area where security would keep out everyone but employees holding official badges. Slipping into the dark glass–tinted Lincoln he'd had his driver pick up, he ordered, "Take the remote routes and make sure we aren't followed."

He swiped the screen of his phone and called his father. The older man picked up on the second ring. "What's going on, Miguel?"

The note of disappointment in his dad's voice worsened the knot of tension in his gut. "It's not my fault this time." He hated having to defend himself.

"I know, son. You've been off their radar for a while now, and I'm proud of you."

Miguel sprang up. Had he heard correctly? "Thanks, Dad. So I'm still in the running for the job?"

Whenever his father used the tactic of elongated silence, Miguel knew he'd better confess all his sins.

"I wasn't seen at those clubs because I was partying. Well, I was, but I was helping out a friend."

The other side of the line remained quiet.

"I'm helping to rebrand her club and she needed to see what successful clubs looked like. I was respecting your mandate by leaving my face out of the cameras. That's why I was wearing the disguise." He finished with his voice low. Would his father believe him or think he'd been trying to put one over on them.

The man's deep chuckle made Miguel wonder if he was still speaking to his father. "I believe you, son. I've witnessed your maturity and I'm proud of you."

Miguel's mouth dropped, dumbfounded that his father had believed him so readily. "Thank you, sir."

"Tell me more about the young woman you were with? Tanya Carrington."

He may as well share the good news. "She's the woman I'm going to marry." Now he had to convince Tanya.

Silence prevailed for a moment. "One of the articles said you met in college. Is this the same young woman you spoke so highly about when you transferred to Ohio State?"

"Yes, sir."

"Then I wish you the best. That year was the calmest you'd ever been in your life. She seems to be a good influence on you."

Miguel laughed. "She definitely is."

"Keep me posted."

Pride filled Miguel as he hung up the phone. A couple of years ago, his father would've read him the riot act. His dad had acknowledged the effort he'd been making to improve his life, to make himself a better man. He just hoped Tanya would be able to recognize the truth, too.

His phone chimed. "Who do I need to sue?" His older brother's voice cut off Miguel's hello.

"I don't know yet, Nardo, but when I do, you'll be the first person I contact," Miguel said, using the much-hated nickname.

Leonardo snorted. "Things are so serious that you're making jokes. I see. Is the woman with you the same one you had Lanelle slaving over financial paperwork for?"

"You know our sister finds it a pleasure to do anything for me. And, yeah, it was business."

Leonardo grunted. "Is this lady still business? That's not what it looked like as I scrolled through the pics of you two. Damn, she used to be one big mama."

Leave it to Leonardo to be crude. And then his brother surprised him. "I remember you telling me stories about her. Even then I could see you really liked and respected her. Way to see into who she really was. I've gotta go." As abruptly as the conversation began, Leonardo hung up.

Only a few more minutes until he'd be able to hold Tanya again. How could he miss her so much when they were apart? As if half of him disappeared until they got back together. It had been the same in college, but his priorities had been messed up back then. He had his head on straight now. Finally.

Josh. He had to call and let his best friend know before he found out through the media. Face-to-face was the manly way to go about it so he FaceTimed his friend and waited for him to pick up. When there was no answer he relaxed. He'd only have to deal with one pissed-off Carrington at a time. Way more than enough.

Chapter 22

Not even an ulcer could make Tanya's stomach feel this torn up inside. What was taking Miguel so long? She'd arrived at his spectacular home about ten minutes ago, but it may as well have been two hours. Desperate to Google herself to see what the hell was going on, she found it more difficult by the second to keep her promise to him. What didn't he want her to see? Unable to sit, she paced the marble hallway.

Thoughts of a sex video from their night in the hotel kept creeping up on her. Neither of them had recorded the encounter, but what if a hotel worker had? Or maybe the articles had mentioned how inappropriate they were for each other, calling her a gold digger, out to get his money.

What could be so bad that he didn't want her to read about it alone? The worst thought imaginable hit and her heart took a deep tumble. What if she'd been the other woman because she wasn't worthy of being his main one? She tried to shake the idea from her head, but it stuck. What could be worse than losing Miguel because he was someone else's man? She could weather through anything. Anything but losing him.

She rotated on her heel as the door swung open and Miguel rushed through. Dropping his briefcase, he ran to her and came to a halt as his large hands touched her face, shoulders, down her arms and then her hips, as if examining her for broken bones before slamming her against his body in the tightest hug she'd ever received.

"If they had hurt you, I would've eradicated all of them."

She used the little air left in her lungs to laugh. "You're a powerful man, but you may be going overboard."

He pulled back and kissed her with an intimate sweetness. She groaned as she forgot the reason for the emergency exodus and returned the erotic circling of his tongue as she tasted Miguel and breathed in the freshness of his cologne.

"I can't believe how much I love you," he said with a last nip of her bottom lip as he moved away. "Remember that."

Was what he had to show her so bad? Her whole body grew cold. "I can't take it anymore. What did they say?"

Tugging at her hand, he went back to the door to pick up his briefcase before leading her into the comfortable book-lined living room. Her belly quaked with trepidation as she watched him pull tabloids from the leather case. She closed her eyes to forestall the inevitable. "It's not just on the net?"

"No. They dug into your, I mean our, past."

Her eyes sprang open and hope flared. They hadn't found anything newsworthy in the present. At least it wasn't about him with another female. She thrust her shoulders back and pretended to have courage as she looked down at one of the papers.

A picture of her staring up into Mr. Coleman's eyes seemed innocuous enough, until she saw the insert picture of them together back in college and then a solitary one of her when she was at her heaviest a year later. Her heart dropped to her toes as the heading hit her—"Miguel Astacio's Charity Case."

She flipped the pages until she got to the article. A wave of nausea hit her as she read. How could they be so cruel? The writer had picked her apart. From her weight to her struggling club, and even intimating that she'd turned her ex-husband onto men. The past she could deal with. She could even live with the lies.

The part where they mentioned Miguel being ashamed to be seen with her as himself made her dizzy with fear. They'd named his aliases and pictured her with them at the clubs. They seemed to gloat when they mentioned that only two months ago he'd been seen in Paris wearing his own face with Sashara Essien, an heiress to an oil empire in Nigeria. The picture showed off Sashara's curvaceous yet thin body wearing a designer gown, looking as if she knew she belonged in it and with Miguel. They were smiling at each other, with Miguel's dimples front and center.

The last part of the article discussed how long her

and Miguel's rags-to-riches romance would last. The author gave it a month because, after all, they did have history. Eventually, he'd find someone of his caliber.

The crushing in her chest prevented her from taking in deep breaths. She covered her mouth as bile rose up. Miguel stood and rushed her out of the living room and to a half bathroom down the hall. She slammed the door shut as she zoned in on the toilet.

Tears stung her eyes as she released the contents of her stomach. Her world was crumbling just like she knew it would. She had no right being with a man like Miguel. They were too different. She retched again, but nothing came out.

A light knock sounded on the door. "Sweetheart, are you okay? Can I come in?"

Horrified, she placed a hand on the door. "No... I just...need a moment." Struggling to take in deep breaths, she waited before rinsing her mouth. Tears streamed down her face. No, she could never compete with Sashara or any of the other glamorous women he'd dated over the years. She was a simple, local girl. She didn't know how to associate with the rich. She'd be a constant embarrassment to him. And herself.

Would the media ever get tired of making fun of the heavyset woman she used to be? Would they always see her as an uncouth, middle-class woman who was out for a hunk of the Astacio fortune?

He claimed to love her, but was he humiliated to be seen with her? Was that *really* why he had to be in disguise every time they were together?

Her pounding head couldn't take anymore. She wanted to go home and hide. Forever. Why had she ever listened to her brother and gone to Miguel for help? Why had she let her pride allow Broderick to goad her into keeping the club instead of selling it and splitting the profits? Why had she fallen in love with Miguel? Again?

The last tore her up the worst. He'd been no good for her the first time. What had made her think anything had changed other than her losing weight and time passing?

She washed her face wishing she could scrub out everything else just as easily. Getting through this without any more pain and mortification was the main thing. No matter how much she'd hoped the fairy-tale dream would come true, Miguel wasn't hers to keep.

Why did the truth have to hurt so damn badly?

She couldn't stay in the bathroom forever. She had to face him, to tell him her final decision. No more making love until she felt as if she'd vanish once they separated. No more pretending to be in a relationship when there was no future for them.

She'd continue to accept the help he'd offered for her club, but she'd cut off anything personal. Just as it should've been in the beginning. Leaving the room to tell him was the hardest thing she'd ever had to do. Why couldn't she have him? She deserved to be happy after all these years. Didn't she?

Who was to say Miguel was her one? *Who's to say he isn't?* her heart whispered. She swallowed the lump in her throat. She could cry all day and night for the rest of her life once she got through this and went home.

After a deep inhale and release of a shaky breath, she opened the door. The sight of Miguel's lips set in a deep frown of worry nearly melted her resolve. She breezed past him as if she were actually confident about her decision. "I'd like to go home now."

He rushed to catch up with her and blocked her path. "Let's talk about it."

"What about?" Cocking her head, she gazed up into his extraordinary eyes. "The media hates me. They think I'm a gold-digging porker who is so far out of your league that they question how I've even managed to bamboozle you. Yet, they're confident you'll wake up and see me for who I really am." She held up a hand to stop him from speaking. "To be honest, I had my doubts about us. We're so different in class that sometimes it makes my heart ache. And there's nothing I can do about it because I am who I am and you're an heir of the great Astacio dynasty." She waved between them. "We were crazy to think this could work."

"Did you have doubts about us back in college?"

She scoffed. "I was young, naive and stupid. I've learned too much since then. Besides nothing came from whatever we shared in the past. You made sure of it."

A twitch appeared in his jaw. "And I explained why. I couldn't lose your brother's friendship at the time, and I was an imbecile. Totally undeserving of you."

She crossed her arms over her chest in an attempt to ward off any more of his tempting words. "And now?"

"I'm still undeserving." He stared into her eyes for the longest time. "But now, I know I can be a good man to you. To treat you like the queen you are."

Dammit. How could he have found the perfect things to say so readily? And then she recalled his marketing guru status. He could get anyone to buy whatever he was selling. A shake of her head helped to clear it. No more falling into him. They had separate lives to lead.

Self-preservation was the key. "The words are nice," she gritted out, "but they aren't enough. You'll get tired of me, just like you did every other woman you've ever been with." She wasn't delusional enough to think she was anything special.

His hands clenched and opened several times as he arched his neck to look up at the ceiling. When his eyes focused back on her, she had to hold her position rather than stumble away from his obvious anger. "You have got to be the most hardheaded woman I have ever met." Rather than argue with her as expected, he swung around and stomped into the living room, leaving her too stunned to follow. When he returned he held her bag. He thrust it at her before heading toward the front door. "Are you coming?"

She blinked several times. Was he letting her go? Just like that? Didn't he know the vultures were out to hound her for a statement? Didn't he care? She no longer had to pretend to be angry because now the edges of her vision had blurred with it as she stomped over his expensive floors to catch up to him while he stood fuming at her with the door open. "What the hell is wrong with you?" she asked in a raised voice. "I'm the one they tore apart in front of the whole world. You came out looking like some kind of benevolent angel showing mercy to a homely, middle-class, stricken, formerly obese woman."

"What pisses me off is that you can't see how much it hurts me to see you in pain." He'd raised his voice to match her volume as his nostrils flared like a bull ready to stomp on anything that got in the way. "You never intended to get involved. I get that. I was a jerk to you in the past. I apologized and I thought we'd gotten past it."

She stood on her toes to get up into his face. His scent distracted her weak self for a moment. "I forgave you. We put it past us."

"That's garbage and you know it." He glared down at her, his eyes dark. "The first chance you got to call off whatever we have going on between us and you're ready to run. You don't trust me as far as you can throw a five-hundred-pound anvil."

That did it. The gloves were off, and they were going to do some MMA. Neither of them would leave this conversation unscathed. "You admitted to choosing my brother over me. How can I trust that if Josh told you today that you should leave me alone that you won't? Or if things get to be too much with the press or your family that you won't leave me? You created your own reputation, Astacio. It's you who doesn't have sticking power."

Creases appeared in the corners of his eyes with his narrowed gaze. "I told you I've changed. You are the one I want to be with. No one else. There's no way I will ever hurt you like that again."

"And what are you going to have them tell the press about me?" She poked a finger into his chest and refrained from wincing at the pain she'd caused herself. "Nothing. It's written all over your shocked face. You weren't planning to tell them anything about me. I was a challenge to you, that's why. You wanted to see if you could get me back after the damage you did. It just *happened* to make you look good in my brother's eyes by helping his sister out."

Raising his hands into the air, his fingers clenched into claws and he growled. "I can't talk to you. Not while you're like this."

"What? Now that I'm being honest?"

"No. You're letting fear rule you. Trying to destroy any chance we have of being together."

His logic penetrated into her brain, but she batted it away. "No, Miguel. We never had a chance. We had an encounter. You knew all along it wasn't long-term. You can't handle it because I'm the one breaking it off this time." She stormed out the door with her nose in the air. She'd walk home if she had to, but she wasn't spending another moment with him in his extravagant house.

He followed her out, grabbed her arm and swung her around. "Where do you think you're going?"

"Home."

A bark of laughter came from his throat. "Are you seriously thinking of walking?"

"God gave me two good legs. If you won't take me there, they will."

The tense stare down ended with him relaxing his flattened lips long enough to say, "Let's go."

She'd won the fight. Why did her plummeting stomach make it feel as if she'd lost everything?

Chapter 23

"I'm shutting the phone off," Tanya told Becca. It had been the longest day of her life. Not just because she couldn't get into her house due to the media presence when Miguel had tried to drop her off earlier, but because she missed him so damn much. It had only been six hours since she'd lost her ever-loving mind and let her deepest, darkest fears win.

Becca picked up the phone and handed it back to Tanya. "You still need to hear from Josh. As soon as he calls you back, you can shut it down. You spoke to your parents and the people who actually care about you and aren't just butting into your business." Becca's brow arched high. "By the way, you don't owe Broderick jack."

"I gathered that when you tried to wrestle the phone from my hands when he called. He was my husband."

"No. He was your roommate."

Too mentally drained to argue, Tanya rested her head on the back of the couch and closed her eyes. She'd told her friend everything that had happened, including the blowout with Miguel. Becca had been uncharacteristically quiet about it and hadn't rendered an opinion.

Between eating her way through Becca's fridge and fretting about having lost Miguel, she'd racked her brain in an effort to find out who'd leaked the information to the media. Who could've had access to the pictures she'd scanned and stored on the cloud? She couldn't see a hacker breaking into her account.

Could it be Broderick? Would he betray her like that? What would he gain? *Money. Lots of it.* But how would he have known about Miguel being in costume? It could've been anyone who had access to her computer, and it didn't help that she used the same password for everything. She'd have to rectify that.

Her cell rang and Becca answered it. Tanya sat in stunned horror as her friend told her brother everything. The whole sordid story, leaving out the amazing sex she'd shared with Miguel.

"I know, right!" Becca exclaimed. "I've been waiting for you. I knew you'd see reason." Her laughter made the hair at the back of Tanya's neck stand on edge. "Yeah. I'm going to put you on speakerphone now."

"Are you there, Tee?"

Tanya glowered at Becca, attempted to snag the phone away and failed. "I'm here," she mumbled.

"Becca tells me you're holding up well."

She shrugged even though she knew he couldn't

see her. "What else can I do under the onslaught of international defamation?"

Her brother laughed. "You'll be all right."

"Now that you know I'm fine, I'm going to shut off the phone so I can get some peace. Everyone I've ever known has been calling. Can you believe that Mom was excited?"

"She's always wanted one of us to be famous. Turns out, it didn't matter how."

A giggle slipped out. There was nothing like talking about parental units with the one person who could understand the most. She loved her brother, but had to get off the phone before the collusion he had with Becca came to light. "Okay, little bro, I'm out. Thanks for checking up on me."

"How are things with Miguel?" Josh asked, ignoring her.

She made sure her voice sounded upbeat. "Great. He's done a fantastic job making the place over. His birthday party is two weekends away and everything is ready." Hopefully, she'd finally get to see her brother after two months of him being in Africa. "Are you coming for his birthday party?"

He grunted. "The man threatened to send a private jet to come get me."

A smile broke through Tanya's misery while Becca laughed.

"My contract ends on Friday, so I'll be there."

She had to keep him distracted so he and Becca couldn't go on the attack. She wouldn't be able to handle both of them at the same time. "Where will you be going next?"

Becca shook her head. "Don't answer, Josh, it's

a diversion. Tell her what we think about how she treated Miguel."

Josh cleared his throat as if uncomfortable with the change in topic. "I was hoping you'd say it and I'd just, um, back you up."

Her best friend glared at the phone. "Fine." She raised her eyes to meet Tanya's. "You're making a horrible mistake. How long have you loved this guy? Since forever, right, Josh?"

"Correct."

Becca tapped her chest. "Even I can see he's changed, and I didn't want you to get involved with him from the get-go. Now I'm on his side. He's good for you. And Lord knows you're good for him."

Josh jumped in with, "The only reason I didn't want him dating you back in college was because he wasn't ready."

"You mentioned this last month," Tanya groused.

"It bears repeating. I'm sorry I got between you two back then, and if I'd known *how* he'd broken off whatever had been starting between you, I would've kicked his ass back then. Or gone to the hospital trying."

Her widened, shocked gaze flew to Becca, who found a sudden interest in her fingernails. When had the little snitch told her brother? "That's in the past and we've gotten over it."

"No, she hasn't. She's petrified it'll happen again," Becca tattled. "And can you believe she thinks her financial status had any bearing on the potential of their relationship?"

"Social standing," Tanya defended. "We're from two different worlds."

"Uranus and Pluto?" Becca deadpanned.

Josh chuckled. "Uranus. Good one, sweets."

Becca and Tanya froze.

"Are you two there?" Josh asked.

Becca swallowed audibly. "You just gave away our secret."

"What?" Tanya's eyes ping-ponged from her best friend to the phone. "You two are together? When? How?" She took a deep breath and started from the beginning. "What?"

Becca patted her on the shoulder. "I'll explain everything later. Right now we have to get your head right about Miguel."

"Uh, yeah," Josh stumbled in. "When I spoke to him earlier, he sounded distraught. I've never heard him like that before. He really thinks he's lost you."

"Wait a minute." Tanya pointed her finger at the phone. "This is the second damn time you've spoken to that man before checking up on me."

"Only by a few minutes. He called me as I was about to dial you."

"Huh." Curiosity got the better of her. "What else did he say?"

"He felt horrible about you being caught in the cross fire. He also mentioned wishing you weren't so stubborn."

Becca giggled. "Don't we all?"

Tanya ignored them as she gnawed on her bottom lip. Would she and Miguel be able to make it as a couple? She loved him, that was for sure. Wasn't love supposed to conquer all? *Just like it had all those years ago?* the demon on her shoulder shouted. Did he love her like he'd claimed? How could she really and truly know?

Wouldn't it be better to play it safe and stay away from him? And possibly never know happiness again? Could she live her life like that? Did she want to?

"He also said he had no clue about who gave the tabloids the information about you. Any idea?"

"I think it's Broderick," Becca said with a snarl.

"Not me," Tanya rushed to say. "What would he have to gain?"

"I don't know, but if it was him, he'd better watch himself because Miguel is on the warpath," Josh said.

"What sage advice did you give him about Tanya?" Becca asked.

"To give her time."

Tanya crossed her arms over her chest, wishing she weren't feeling so out of sorts. She and Miguel weren't meant to be together and she had to get used to it. "Will it change our social standings?"

"You never know," Josh replied. "Listen, I've gotta go. Both of you be safe. Call Miguel if you need anything. I'll see you in a few days. I love you."

"Love you, too," she and Becca said in unison. Every muscle in Tanya's face went lax as she stared at her best friend. While one love had been lost, another had been found.

Chapter 24

Miguel didn't care that he knocked loud enough to wake everyone in the ritzy condo Tanya's club manager lived in. Clint Davis, the rat bastard who'd informed the tabloids about him and Tanya, had made a detrimental mistake in his little venture. He hadn't sold the information to the highest bidder, but to many.

It had only taken a few phone calls to get the name of the informant. The editors were pissed. Not that Miguel felt badly for the garbage-picking vultures.

The door swung open and it was all he could do not to plant his fist in the smirking man's face. "To what do I owe this visit, Mr. Astacio?"

Why had Tanya defended him so staunchly? Loyalty was one thing, but being blind to a person's true nature could be dangerous. He didn't need the reason behind why Clint had betrayed someone who'd considered him a friend. All he knew was that his actions had revealed the nastiness he consisted of. "If I ever catch you in Tanya's club again—"

The man stood to his full height and stepped to him. "What? You're all costumes and talk. Did you think you were fooling me with your weak getup, Isaac Graham? I'm smarter than that. I confirmed it when Broderick's prissy ex-wife spoke to you on the phone and called you by your last name." His gaze rode to the left of Miguel. "You can't even come up in here like a man. You need security for backup." One step closer brought him right into Miguel's face.

He let his bodyguard pull him back. The scumbag wasn't worth getting into a fight with.

"Why couldn't you just screw her, fix the club and leave well enough alone? Your little influence over her ruined my money," Clint spit out. "I didn't have to blackmail her like I did Broderick, though I didn't have anything on her. Besides, I had her wrapped around my finger." He grunted. "I should've had those full lips wrapped around my di—"

Miguel lost it. Leaping toward the prick, he would've had him by the throat if the guy hadn't had such quick reflexes and his security hadn't caught him just in time.

Clint held both hands to his own neck, mouth open, finally gaining a clue about what Miguel was capable of.

Flexing his hands, Miguel did his best to calm down by counting his deeply inhaled breaths. If he'd made contact, he would've seriously hurt the scumbag and possibly ended up arrested, but for Tanya, he'd move the world. He just wished she understood.

Straightening the lapels on his wool coat, Miguel scanned the weasel from head to toe and spoke in the crisp tone that let people know his jovial temperament had disappeared. "As I was saying. If you step foot in her club or restaurant again…" He let the words hang as he cocked his head.

He didn't have the shark reputation of his older brother, but he'd been known to shake down an individual a time or two. Maybe Clint had heard the rumors because he slunk back. With one last stare and not another wasted word, Miguel turned on his heel and walked away, leaving his bodyguard to watch his back.

Sitting behind the wheel of his Maserati, the tires screeched as he took off. In a useless attempt to burn through his adrenaline and frustration with Tanya, he banked the corner hard and fast only to slam his brakes when a motorcycle got in his way. At the sight of Roland grasping the dashboard and the tough man's light brown skin a little paler than when they'd gotten into the car, Miguel released a chuckle. "You can relax now. I'll slow down."

True to his word, he took the route home at a more sedate speed.

He'd told Tanya who was behind the media blitz as soon as he'd made the discovery. For once, she hadn't argued when he said he'd take care of it. Miguel scrubbed a hand through his curls. "What the hell am I going to do about my woman?" Not only was Roland on retainer as one of the most effective bodyguards in his employ, but he considered him a friend and would bounce ideas off him every once in a while. He already knew everything going on with Tanya. The guy had a good head on his shoulders.

Roland shrugged. "Her brother told you to wait her out. Since he knows her the best, I'd follow his suggestion."

Not what he wanted to hear. How long was he supposed to sit in this state of limbo before Tanya figured out that the differences in their finances didn't matter? He had enough to share, especially since she tended to decline what he offered her. At least she'd met with him over the week to put the finishing touches on the club, even if things were awkward between them.

He had no idea how to make things right. How had he survived all those years without her when each moment made him feel raw and on edge?

Roland rubbed his goatee. "A big gesture never hurts. It always gets me out of the doghouse with my wife."

He'd thought the same thing, but everything he came up with would get thrown back in his face. "She's not a gift person."

"Every female likes presents, man. You just have to know your woman and get her the right one."

Did he know Tanya well enough to be able to persuade her with something that would let her know how much he wanted to be with her? Short of giving away all his money and becoming a recluse, he had no idea how to equalize their statuses. Neither of them would be happy with that, but if it was what she needed in order to know how much he loved her, then he would. For the woman his body, mind and heart had decided on, he'd do anything.

* * *

Tanya smoothed down the body-hugging rust-colored dress with the plunging back. She felt like she'd worn more with a towel wrapped around her than she did in this dress. Mentally wincing at the hit her credit card had taken when she'd ordered it from the Astacio clothing line, she smiled at her reflection in the VIP lounge's glass divider where she did her best to make sure everything was in order. Miguel had spoiled her for anything that wasn't quality.

She'd decided to show off her figure, just because she could. It had nothing to do with loving the way Miguel's eyes had bugged out when he'd first come into the club. His birthday party was in full swing and although she'd caught the eye of some of the superstar friends he'd invited, he was the only one she had spent the night maneuvering herself to get glimpses of.

Being around people she'd seen only on television, movies or the internet reiterated the imbalance of their lives. She might currently look cool and composed, but she'd had her moment of screams and giggles with Becca in her office earlier.

Her best friend had tagged up with Josh over the past week when he'd arrived to influence her to change her mind. Not even she knew what was holding her back. She loved Miguel, of that she had no doubt. He loved her, too. Believing it wasn't difficult, but would she be enough for him? Her self-doubt kept her away from her heart's desire.

The past week of working with him but not being able to let go and be herself had been torture. And now even their friendship was at stake. It didn't matter that he'd achieved their goal and made Fervor the hottest club in Cleveland, at least for the night.

He'd even taken care of that weasel Clint for her, for which she'd been very grateful because she might have ended up in jail if she'd ever had to see him again. Brittany, the new club manager she'd hired, was full of new ideas on how to keep the place hot and vibrant.

A deep inhale fortified Tanya with the courage to go up to Miguel's gorgeous sister, who sat relaxing in the crook of her husband's arm. "Hi, Lanelle, I know we've never met, but I'm—"

Lanelle grabbed Tanya's hand and pulled her down to sit by her side on the couch. "Tanya Carrington." Would she make a joke about her losing tons of weight or entering the eye of the paparazzi like some of the other stars had done? She'd never let anyone know, but she got a head rush anytime someone recognized her. If only it had been for something she'd actually accomplished in her life.

"Miguel talks about you all the time. Ever since he met you in college."

What response could she give? She smiled and recalled the reason she'd come to the woman. "Thank you for working on the financials of the club."

Lanelle waved down a hand. "No problem." She turned to the man at her side and said, "Babe, this is the woman who has Miguel's nose hooked and open. This is my husband, Dante Sanderson."

The long-legged dark man whose handsomeness rivaled the models packing the place reached out a hand with a wide smile. "Pleasure to meet you. He's even spoken to me about you—trying to figure out how to get out of the doghouse."

Heat torpedoed to her face and she wanted to run and hide until the embarrassment faded. She forced herself to shake Dante's hand. "Nice to meet you, too."

Before she could say another word, a man the size of a professional football player stood in front of their couch and held out a hand to her. "We need to have a talk. Let's dance."

Tanya blinked up at him. Lanelle saved her from having to tell him off, in a nice way of course, by giggling. "What the hell happened to those etiquette classes Mom made you take all those years ago? Still haven't caught, have they?" She rested a hand on Tanya's shoulder. "This is our older brother, Leonardo. He never really learned how to get along with the human race."

Tanya's laugh was more of a nervous giggle as Leonardo waited for her. She stuck her nose in the air. "If you *ask* me, I might consider it."

The couple jeered. "Way to go," Lanelle said.

Probably not used to having his requests denied, he seemed to expand before he said, "Will you dance with me?"

No *please*, but at least he hadn't growled the question. She placed her fingers in his hand only to have them engulfed when he pulled her up. He guided her toward the rail, instead of down the stairs, where they could look out over the partygoers while showing off their dance moves. Leonardo didn't attempt to dance. "My brother is a good man."

Shocked at his opening statement, she hung on to the rail, the beat pulsing into her hand. "Yes, he is."

He leveled her with an intense stare of his dark eyes. He and Miguel were different, but the family resemblance could be seen in the shape of the eyes and mouth. "So what's the problem? You liked him in college and he's become an even better person since then. I did a background check on you and you're a genuinely hard worker who tends to keep to herself. With the way you've been staring at him all night, I believe you like my brother. I don't understand what's holding you back." He looked at her unblinking as if he'd asked a question and awaited an answer.

Unbalanced, she applied even more of her weight onto the metal as she attempted to figure out how to get the hell out of there.

Miguel sidled up to her. "Sorry to interrupt your little chat, Nardo, but I'm stealing Tanya away."

It wasn't relief that made her heart crash against the inside of her chest. Miguel was stunning in a hunter-green suit that showed off his wide muscular shoulders and lean hips. The slim black tie gave him a modern edge. Her nipples puckered at the sight of his plump lips and his freshly shaved face. All natural. Her favorite look. It had been too long since she'd touched him. Whose fault was that? *Destiny's.*

She couldn't get out of there fast enough when she turned to the large scowling Astacio. "Um, nice to meet you, Leonardo."

Miguel wrapped an arm around her waist and her traitorous body melted into him as his warmth seeped into her. Damn, she'd missed him. "Call him Nardo. He loves it."

Leonardo growled as they made their way down the stairs amid pats on the back and birthday shout-outs to Miguel.

Coming to her senses, she attempted to wiggle

away, but he held her tight against him. Her body didn't want to leave him anyway, so she didn't struggle as they crawled through the party. "Is he always so...intense?" she yelled into his ear.

Miguel nodded. "When he's on a mission, which is all the time. He's the oldest and had to deal with issues Lanelle and I didn't."

"Oh." And then a second later, she furrowed her brows, not having a clue about what growing up must have been like for the man. "I'm the oldest, too. I had to take the brunt of my parents' learning strategies and I'm, um, not like that."

"There's more to Leonardo than meets the eye."

"I'll take your word for it."

He laughed as they entered her office. "My parents couldn't make it tonight. They're flying in from a business trip, but my mother has a family dinner arranged for tomorrow evening." He paused and added, "I'd like you to join us."

Moving away, she started to decline the invitation to the intimate event, but he stopped her by placing his hands on her shoulders. Before she knew it, he had dipped his head down and brushed his soft lips against hers.

An electric current flared through her as she clung to him. She'd missed his mouth gliding expertly on hers, the scent of citrus and sandalwood making her draw him deeper into her, and his incredible taste. Cognac and Miguel. Sexy as hell. She couldn't stop her tongue from tangling with his when he entered her mouth with a moan.

Catching herself before she could unbutton his shirt to feel his warm skin against her greedy palms, she pulled away. It took more than one try, but she found the strength to do it. Breathing heavily, she stumbled back. Since her legs no longer possessed the ability to support her, she ungraciously folded her body onto the couch.

The effort to speak after such a body-rattling kiss was monumental, so she allowed the silence to stir between them for a few moments before she raised her head and found his gaze. "What did you call me in here for?"

His extraordinary hazel eyes stared into hers, making her ache with a deep need. "I'm going to rip a page from my brother's book and skip the charm." He grinned. "It never worked on you anyway."

For the first time since the media had ruined her life, a genuine smile touched her lips while around him.

Sitting beside her, he grabbed her hands and rubbed her knuckles. Seeking his touch, she didn't pull away. "Have you gotten over your issue of me having money?"

She tried to slide her hands out of his grip, but he wouldn't allow it. "It's not about money. It's more that we run in different social circles."

He arched a brow. "Do you hang out with humans?"

"Yes," she drawled, unsure where he was taking the discussion.

"Then we have no problem. I watched you interacting with the biggest names in the industry out there. You didn't bat an eye."

She giggled. "You didn't see me and Becca in here releasing all of our excitement a couple of hours ago."

His eyes twinkled. "You're a class act. There's nothing and no one you can't handle."

Her heart swelled so much at the faith he had in her, she feared it would burst. Confidence was an incredibly easy thing to knock down, but building it took time and an awful lot of energy. Did he really think she could blend into his world when she'd barely been able to fit into her own?

"I have a proposition for you."

She turned her head and looked at him out of the corners of her eyes, hesitant to discover what this creative man had come up with. "What?"

"Since giving up my money is—"

"The dumbest idea ever," she interjected with an extreme eye roll.

Raising his hand, he brushed a strand of hair behind her ear and stroked the back of his fingers along her cheek, sending her body into an overheated tizzy. "But giving you up is even stupider. Impossible, actually."

She blinked several times as tears stung the backs of her eyes.

"So I've found a way to equalize things." He reached into his pocket and pulled something out as he bent down onto one knee.

She cupped a hand over her mouth when he opened the box to expose a brilliant diamond flanked on the sides by amethysts. Her birthstone. After all these years, he'd remembered.

"Tanya Portia Carrington, I have loved you from the first time you told me off in college. With every moment I spent with you back then, I fell deeper. In the years we've been apart, no woman could measure up to you and I refused to settle."

Were those tears in his eyes, or was her own blurred vision making her see things?

"I was stupid to let you go. I'm smarter than I was back then and refuse to ever let it happen again. Your fear of us being different is unfounded, but I'd like to even things out by giving you everything I have. Will you marry me, and be my partner in life? For richer and richer?"

She pressed her hands against her chest. Never in her life had she expected such beautiful words to be spoken to her, much less by the man she loved with all her heart. Debilitating fear popped up to the surface, making her sweat. She wanted to say yes. With every experience they'd ever shared, with every cell in her body, she wanted to say yes.

"Before you answer, I have one last thing for you." He placed the box in her palm and closed her trembling fingers over it before standing and reaching for her.

Too overwhelmed to speak, she allowed him to take her out of her office and to the main dance floor. The party was going strong with Kiwi putting on the performance to end all shows. They walked to the front and he waved to Kiwi.

Was he going to make a speech? Her face went hot as she tugged at his arm to pull him back. She wouldn't be able to withstand the mortification if he announced their issues in front of everyone. And, besides, she had chosen him.

Marrying him soon was out of the question when they still had a lot to learn about each other, but the fact that he wanted to have her as his wife one day made her feel as if heaven had come to earth.

Kiwi smiled and nodded at Miguel before giving the DJ a thumbs-up. A moment later, the song changed. Tanya recognized it with a few notes. She lost it when Kiwi started singing. Tears streamed down her cheeks. He'd remembered.

Kiwi handed him the microphone during the chorus. In his rough voice, he sang the lyrics to her favorite Mary J. Blige song about being devoted to another and their relationship being strong. Back in college, it had reminded her of what she'd wanted with Miguel, and she'd played it over and over again even though everyone complained. The lyrics had spoken to her, deep inside her soul. What she wouldn't have given to have him return her feelings because she'd loved him so much.

She snatched the microphone from him and flung it back to Kiwi, not only to save the crowd from his horrible singing, but to jump onto him screaming, "Yes, Miguel. Yes."

It took him a surprised moment to understand the meaning of her response, and then he kissed her hard while twirling them around.

What had she almost given up because she'd thought herself inadequate for him? Her heart. Her destiny.

"I love you so much," she said as joy overflowed. The crowd cheered as Kiwi continued to sing the song that would always be theirs.

He settled her on her feet, released the ring box from her hand and took out the exquisite piece of jewelry. At that point, even if he'd given her a rubber arm bracelet, she would've thought it was perfect.

Grinning down at her, he mouthed as he slid the ring onto her finger, "Equals?"

She nodded with the biggest smile. "Forever."

Epilogue

"Are you sure you want to sell the club?" Miguel asked as they went through the contract together in his living room. "To Broderick, of all people?" The twitch in his jaw had never gone away when her ex-husband's name came up. The day Miguel and Broderick had met, she'd been sure Miguel's jaw would be permanently clenched by the time the encounter ended.

Even after six months of basically living with him because they hated being apart, she still couldn't believe he was hers. She nodded. "More than ready. Broderick can handle the place, especially since we're getting a hefty profit from the sale. We've done what we set out to do and made Fervor number one. I'm ready to branch out and do something I've wanted to do for a while now."

Miguel grinned. "Expand your restaurant like you've talked about."

"Yes. I can't believe you let Broderick have the name 'Fervor.'"

He laughed. "We can't snatch the brand away from him. Besides, the process of you coming up with a new name for your restaurant will give me an endless amount of amusement."

She slapped his shoulder. "Ha-ha. You're one funny man, Mr. Astacio."

"I like to think so."

"But there's another reason I'm ready to sell the club."

"What's that?"

She couldn't wipe the smile off her face. "So I can help plan our wedding. I'm not fool enough to think I can't do it without a wedding planner. I'm ready to marry the most incredible, generous, caring, loving, fantastic lover in the—"

Once her words seemed to register, Miguel leaped up and landed on top of her, smothering her with kisses all over her face. And then he slowed down with a sultry passion-filled kiss before coming up for air. "When?"

Holding his face between her hands, she would rather have continued the journey of the kiss. "Is six months too soon?"

He turned his head and rubbed his lips on her palm. "Not soon enough for me. If you said tomorrow I'd be game."

She laughed. "And disallow the world from witnessing the wedding of the Executive Public Relations Officer of Astacio Enterprises? Never." She was immensely proud of him. Not only did he work the hell out of his new position, but because he was so exceptional at marketing, his father insisted he maintain the one as marketing director. And he still made time to pamper her. She'd be marrying an amazing man and she'd never forget it.

"Tomorrow is soon enough to start planning." He bent and nibbled her neck, making her moan and hold him closer. "Tonight I want to celebrate the fact that I'm marrying the woman I have and always will love."

* * * * *

KIMANI ROMANCE

COMING NEXT MONTH
Available August 21, 2018

#585 A STALLION DREAM
The Stallions • by Deborah Fletcher Mello

Collin Stallion plans to give back to the community by volunteering to exonerate someone wrongfully convicted of a crime. His partner in the high-profile case, powerhouse attorney London Jacobs, isn't impressed by the Stallion. Until passion ignites. But with adversaries looming, will they fulfill their dream of love?

#586 LOVE FOR ALL TIME
Sapphire Shores • by Kianna Alexander

Sapphire Shores is rolling out the red carpet for Sierra Dandridge—the "ice queen." But real estate scion Campbell Monroe finds nothing cold about the worldly beauty. Their desire culminates in an intimate affair. Until a younger actress's vicious social media campaign threatens Sierra's career and life…

#587 THE HEIRESS'S SECRET ROMANCE
The Kingsleys of Texas • by Martha Kennerson

Investigator Kathleen Winston's task is clear: uncover the truth about the alleged safety violations at Kingsley Oil and Gas. But one look at ruggedly sexy VP Morgan Kingsley and her scrutiny transforms into seduction! But can the emotionally guarded bachelor forgive Kathleen once her identity—and her heart— are revealed?

#588 WINNING HER FOREVER
Bay Point Confessions
by Harmony Evans

Construction entrepreneur Trent Waterson has a passion for hard work…and the one woman in Bay Point who tries to avoid him. Former dancer Sonya Young is stunned to learn that Trent's brother is scheming to buy her childhood home. Can Trent choose between family loyalty and their breathtaking chemistry?

Get 4 FREE REWARDS!

We'll send you 2 FREE Books plus 2 FREE Mystery Gifts.

Harlequin® Desire books feature heroes who have it all: wealth, status, incredible good looks... everything but the right woman.

FREE
Value Over
$20

Collin Stallion was sheer perfection, she thought as she stared in his direction. He'd changed into a casual suit of polished sateen. It was expertly tailored with clean, modern lines and fitted him exceptionally well. The color was a rich, deep burgundy and he wore a bright white T-shirt beneath it. He'd changed his shoes as well, a pair of pricey white Jordan sneakers now adorning his feet. He'd released his dreadlocks and the sun-kissed strands hung down his back past his broad shoulders. The thick tresses gave him a lionlike mane and he had the look of

a regal emperor. He was too damn pretty and attracting a wealth of attention.

As their gazes locked and held, London felt her cheeks heat with color. Something she didn't recognize pulsed deep in her feminine core and the look he was giving her seemed to tease every ounce of her sensibilities. His eyes were intoxicating, their color a rich amber with flecks of gold that shimmered beneath the setting sun. There was something behind his stare that was heated, igniting a wealth of ardor in the pit of her stomach.

"Collin, hey!" she exclaimed as she reached his side. "I apologize. I didn't mean to be late. I hope you haven't been waiting here long."

He shook his head. "You're fine. You're right on time. I was actually early."

London nodded, suddenly feeling completely out of sorts. She was beyond nervous, her knees beginning to quiver ever so slightly. She felt him sense the rise of discomfort, his own anxiousness dancing sweetly with hers.

He took a deep breath. "Why don't we go inside. I'm sure our table is ready for us," he said as he pressed a gentle hand against the small of her back.

A jolt of electricity shot through London's body at his touch, the intensity of it feeling like she'd combusted from the inside out. It took everything in her not to trip across the threshold of the restaurant's front door.

Don't miss A Stallion Dream
by Deborah Fletcher Mello, available September 2018
wherever Harlequin® Kimani Romance™
books and ebooks are sold.

Want to give in to temptation with
steamy tales of irresistible desire?

Check out **Harlequin® Presents®**, **Harlequin® Desire** and **Harlequin® Kimani™ Romance** books!

New books available every month!

CONNECT WITH US AT:

Harlequin.com/Community

Facebook.com/HarlequinBooks

Twitter.com/HarlequinBooks

Instagram.com/HarlequinBooks

Pinterest.com/HarlequinBooks

ReaderService.com

**ROMANCE WHEN
YOU NEED IT**

PGENRE2017

A flash of lightning outside was followed by an almost
immediate crack of deafeningly loud thunder that made her
jump. She thought she caught a glimpse of a shadow outside
her window, a human-sized shape in the tree, as if someone
had climbed it and was peering inside.

Ohmigod.

She bolted out of bed and flew out of her room, shooting
across the hall to leap into Bastien's room in about one second
flat. She plastered her back against the door, breathing hard.

Bass was out of bed and standing in front of her in about
the same amount of time. Crud, that man could move fast.
"What's wrong?" he bit out.

"I thought I saw someone outside my window. It was
nothing, I'm sure, but it spooked me."

He touched his throat with a finger and ordered tersely,
"I need someone to check out Carrie's room, inside and out,

ASAP. She thought she might have seen someone outside her window."

"Who are you talking to?" she asked.

"My men. We're all wearing earbuds and microphones."

"You went full commando in a bed-and-breakfast? Isn't that a tiny bit of overkill?"

"What if there really is a guy outside your room?" Bass responded.

Oh, God. There went her pulse again.

Bass gathered her into his arms as if he sensed her panic. "I've got you. You're safe. No one's going to hurt you."

She mumbled against his chest, "I feel so stupid."

"No need. You have every reason to be jumpy." A pause, then he added, "You're freezing. Come get under the covers and warm up."

He deposited her in his bed, which was still warm from his body. Heat wrapped round her like the hug he'd just given her, comforting and secure. She was disappointed when he didn't join her. Instead, he continued to stand over by the door, listening at the panel.

Without warning, he slipped outside, leaving her alone in his room. Great. Now she could freak herself out in here.

She stared fixedly at the alarm clock on his nightstand, her tension climbing with every passing minute. What was going on out there? Why had he bolted out of the room like that?

The door flew open and she froze in terror, her gaze darting around frantically in search of a weapon.

Find out who just burst in the door in
Navy SEAL Cop *by Cindy Dees,*
available August 2018 wherever
Harlequin® Romantic Suspense *books and ebooks are sold.*

www.Harlequin.com

Need an adrenaline rush from nail-biting tales
(and irresistible males)?

Check out **Harlequin® Intrigue®**
and **Harlequin® Romantic Suspense** books!

New books available every month!

CONNECT WITH US AT:

Harlequin.com/Community

 Facebook.com/HarlequinBooks

Twitter.com/HarlequinBooks

Instagram.com/HarlequinBooks

Pinterest.com/HarlequinBooks

ReaderService.com

**ROMANCE WHEN
YOU NEED IT**

SGENRE2017